MW00468549

LOVE, UTLEY

LOVE LETTERS BOOK ONE

S.J. TILLY

Love, Utley
Love Letters Series Book One
Copyright © S.J. Tilly LLC 2024
All rights reserved.
First published in 2024
No part of this book may be reproduced, stored in a retrieval system, or transmitted in any form or by any means, without the prior permission in writing of the publisher, nor be otherwise circulated in any form of binding or cover other than that in which it is published and without a similar condition, including this condition, being imposed on the subsequent purchaser. All characters in this publication other than those clearly in the public domain are fictitious, and any resemblance to real persons, living or dead, is purely coincidental.
Cover: Lori Jackson Design
Model Image: Wander Aguiar Photography
Editors: Jeanine Harrell, Indie Edits with Jeanine
& Beth Lawton, VB Edits

This book is dedicated to every woman who has ever had to work with a man.

PROLOGUE – HANNAH

The heavy door slams closed behind me, echoing through the dorm hallway, but I'm too elated to care.

Last night...

Kicking my shoes off, I aim straight for my bed and flop onto my back.

Maddox Lovelace.

Football player extraordinaire.

The tall, broad, dark-haired, dark-eyed man who has been on my mind since the first moment I saw him earlier this week.

The charismatic athlete I'm quickly becoming obsessed with.

The man everyone calls Mad Dog, even though I've already seen a softer side to him.

I sigh.

Never in my wildest dreams did I think my first week at college would go like this.

I mean, sure, I did two years of college already, but that was living at home and going to the cheapest local community college. This is university life. HOP University. And hot damn, has it lived up to its name.

I curl my fingers around the fabric of the borrowed hoodie I'm wearing and bring it up to my nose.

Since Maddox knows I have it, and he let me wear it out of the library, I'm not going to feel weird about inhaling his scent off it.

Even though, from the way I spent the night plastered to his side, my own shirt probably smells like him.

Soap, fresh-cut grass, and sandalwood.

Heaven.

I know I should change. Should probably shower too. But exhaustion from lack of sleep is creeping in, and it's much more fun to lie here and think about last night.

Thinking about Maddox coming to the library.

How he sat there waiting for my shift to end, asking if I'd like to study with him.

Going to that private study room on the second floor.

The kiss.

I let my eyes close.

That kiss was the best kiss of my life.

Or best kiss of my life until later.

Until we lost track of time — me reading from *The Count of Monte Cristo* out loud, him with his head on my shoulder following along.

Until the lights went off.

Until we were locked in.

Heat unfurls in my belly as I remember that moment. The tension between us grew so fast it crackled when we tested the front doors of the library and found them locked.

I've seen it in movies.

Read about it in books.

THE LETTER

Dear Maddox,

I'm sorry to give you a note like this, but I don't want to leave without telling you where I'm going. And I can't leave without letting you know how much last night meant to me. Not just the locked-in part, but all the stuff that came before it too.

Being around you makes me feel safe. Like I'm protected from anything bad. And you... You make me feel small in a world where I've always felt too big.

And I know we just met, and I know it will be hard to do long distance, but I'd like to try. I'd like to still see you. Or at least talk to you.

I hate that we never exchanged phone numbers. I assumed we'd have time to do it later. But

since my time has run out, here is my number.
651-555-1304

There's no easy way to say this next part, so I'll just do it.

My mom had a stroke last night and is in the hospital. They say she'll be okay, but I need to move back home to help her run our store.

And I don't think I'll be able to come back.

I've already emailed my adviser to drop my classes. I've packed up everything in my dorm room. And by the time you're reading this, I'll either be at the bus stop outside the quad or back home in St. Paul.

I don't want to go.

And the biggest reason I want to stay is you.

I'll miss running into you. Miss you catching me when I fall off step stools. Miss hearing you call me Bunny. Miss reading to you.

We could still do that last one over the phone. Which isn't as good as sitting side by side, but it's better than nothing.

I'm sorry again for how sudden this is. But I hope you understand. And I hope you call.

Love,

Utley

ONE

HANNAH – 15 YEARS LATER

"Knock, knock." The man's voice cuts through the silence in my office.

"Hi, Brandon." I greet him, typing out the last line of an email.

When I hit send, I look up from my computer.

Brandon is... okay. Cute in a middle-aged, *I wear fleece vests as a fashion statement* kind of way. But he's not my preferred brand. No matter how many times he not-so-subtly tries to ask me to dinner. Or drinks. Or to his lake house for the weekend.

Even though we both know our salaries don't allow us to purchase second residences. Which means he's referring to his parents' house over on Darling Lake. And I don't know what I dislike more, the way he bends the truth or the cologne he wears.

Taking a calming breath, I remind myself that I'm extra stressed today and that he's not that bad.

I force a smile on my face. "What's up?"

Brandon props his shoulder against my doorframe. "Have you had your interview yet?"

And there it is, the reason for my stress. "Not yet."

The company I've worked at for years was just purchased by another company.

We knew it was a possibility. That the owners had been *considering selling.* But Monday's email told us the deal had been finalized and signed that morning. And that we were all now employees of MinneSolar because our company was being absorbed by this new one.

And if that wasn't terrifying enough, the email also stated that we would be reinterviewing with the new executive team for our current jobs on Wednesday. Today.

My manager told me not to worry about it. That it's standard procedure and more of a way for the new brass to get to know the employees.

But if that was true, I don't think they'd call them interviews. It would just be a meeting.

"I just finished mine," Brandon says, referring to his interview. "Wasn't too bad."

"Did they take the whole forty minutes?" I ask.

He makes a face. "Pretty much. But the questions seemed standard. Didn't feel like they were trying to trip me up or anything."

"That's good." A bit of my anxiety melts away. "Is it really three people at once?"

Brandon's been here since I started four years ago. I know he'll stand there talking whether I ask questions or not, so I might as well ask.

"Yeah. The new CEO seems alright. I think her name was Dana. And the CFO dude was pretty chill. But the last guy." He rolls his eyes. "He didn't even say anything."

"Who was the last guy?" I can tell Brandon doesn't like him, so now I'm intrigued.

"The owner." He scoffs as if he wouldn't love to own a multimillion-dollar company.

"He can't be that bad if he didn't say anything," I try to point out.

Brandon lifts the shoulder he's not leaning on. "I mean, I guess it'd be worse if he was trying to grill me about my position. Considering he probably knows nothing about it."

Ah, yes, there is the obnoxious man I know.

"If he owns the company, I'm sure he gets the basics." I try to keep my annoyance out of my tone.

Brandon is a sales guy, not a freaking mechanical engineer. It's absurd to assume the owner of the company couldn't keep up with his day-to-day selling of solar energy equipment.

I'm an internal auditor. My job is a bit more nuanced, but it really just boils down to me overseeing accounts and expenses. If this guy has enough money to own a solar company large enough to buy and absorb our company, then I'm sure he understands money. Probably even better than I do.

"Maybe," Brandon says skeptically. "But he's only been in the business for like two years. Before that, he played football."

A small chill creeps up the back of my neck, and I sit up straighter in my chair. "What do you mean he played football?"

Brandon glances over his shoulder to check that the hallway is clear, then steps farther into my office. "Have you not heard who the owner is?"

I slowly shake my head. "No. Who is it?"

"It's Mad Dog Maddox. He was the defensive tackle for us for like five years. And before that, he played for Arizona for —"

I don't hear any more of what Brandon says because my ears are filled with a high-pitched ringing sound.

Mad Dog Maddox.

Maddox Lovelace.

The Maddox.

The Maddox I spent one life-altering night with in college.

The man who swept me off my feet, literally, and more than once, only to never ever call.

The one whose career I followed closer than I'll ever admit.

The Maddox I forced myself to stop looking up when he retired from football.

The man who broke my twenty-year-old heart.

The one I've thought of too many times over the past fifteen years.

That Maddox.

That Maddox is here.

"Hannah?" My manager's voice cuts through the noise in my head.

I blink and find her standing behind Brandon in my doorway.

She smiles, unaware that my mental stability is rapidly unraveling. "You're up."

I swallow and nod. "Okay."

She moves away from my door as I push out of my desk chair.

Brandon is still here, taking up space. He says something about luck before finally turning around and exiting, leaving me alone in my office.

Maddox is here.

I take a breath.

You can do this.

I take a second breath.

You're a bad bitch.

I clench my jaw.

You deserve this position.

I unclench my jaw.

You've worked your ass off since...

I take a deep breath in through parted lips.

I've worked my ass off every day of my fucking life to get to where I am.

I moved back home after that one week of living on campus.

I went from the prospect of student life to working full time — scratch that, overtime — at Petals.

I spent my days in the flower shop and my evenings attending online classes to finish my bachelor's degree in accounting. And what was supposed to take me three semesters at HOP U ended up taking me five long years.

Five years of worrying about paying the mortgage. Worrying about Mom's medical bills and the cost of physical therapy. And when it finally seemed like we might have a handle on things, have a plan, my cousin died, and everything changed again. Giving me even bigger worries and responsibilities.

I spent five years under crushing stress as I watched Maddox graduate from college. Get drafted into the NFL. Play his rookie season in Arizona. Go to the playoffs in his second season. Play in the Super Bowl in his third season.

I watched him excel.

I watched him guest anchor for college games.

I watched him living his best life.

Blinking, I tip my head back toward the ceiling.

Keep it together, Hannah.

None of this is new. His success isn't new.

And I'm over him.

It was one stupid week.

One stupid week, a lifetime ago, that I clung to for way too long because I was struggling.

Because I wanted to believe in a different outcome.

Because a stupid, foolish part of me held on to this sliver of hope for years that he might call.

That one day, my phone would ring, and he'd apologize for not calling sooner. That he'd explain how he read the note so many times the numbers smudged on the page. How he tried every combination until he finally got me.

I blink again.

It was irrational.

After the first two weeks passed without a word, I should have let it go.

But I was young. And I wanted someone to save me.

I blink again and remind myself that I'm past all that.

Because I am.

I just never thought I'd have to see him again.

And certainly not like this. Interviewing for my own job.

Taking another breath, I accept the humor in my situation.

I followed Maddox's career in the media for so long. Stemmed from some sort of masochist nature, I guess. And it wasn't until he retired that I decided I needed to stop. Needed to stop caring. Which was good for my mental health. I haven't thought of him in... I don't know how long. But had I continued to follow him, my unprepared ass would've known he was the owner of MinneSolar.

Or, at the very least, I should've spent some of the last two days researching the company rather than being so focused on double-checking all my previous work, wanting my records to be squeaky clean.

A door shuts somewhere down the hall, reminding me of where I am. And what I need to do.

I force my shoulders to relax.

I have a bit of savings now. Not much, but enough to get us through a month or two if I lose my position.

way home means that the interview either went really well or..."

I take another pull of the frothy goodness while I decide how to answer.

"Uh-oh." Chelsea makes a face at Mom as she lays another wide strip of pasta in the pan.

"It was fine," I say before they can start with their theories. "I still have my job. Nothing is changing."

"And you're not happy about that because...?" Mom raises a brow at me.

If I could, I would play it all off. I'd tell them nothing. Pretend nothing was amiss. And go on with life as usual.

But I'm not good at pretending. I can fake it for an interview. Or a brief interaction. But I can't pull it off long term. And I'd rather be honest now than have it all come out later.

They're both staring at me.

"I know the owner. And —" I stop there.

And what? I don't hate him. Not really. I don't even know him. Not anymore. Plus, there's no reason to believe he'll even be in the office that much.

Or... will he?

Dammit, I should have asked around. Figured out if he's the type of owner who actually works at the company or if he just shows up every once in a while to *check on his investment*.

He wasn't interacting in the interview before Peter said my last name, but maybe he was dealing with something important on his phone.

Or maybe he was being a dick.

How am I supposed to know?

"Uh, Grandma. I think someone needs to reset Aunt Hannah."

"Maybe we should add a little extra cheese to the top layer," Mom replies. "That might help."

I snort. "You two are ridiculous."

"And you're glitching like a robot in a rainstorm," Chelsea retorts.

"I think I preferred you as a baby who couldn't talk back."

She laughs. "No way. Babies are gross."

I have to nod my agreement, because they kinda are.

And to be fair, when Chelsea came to live with us, she was already two, so more a toddler than an infant.

"Oh, stop it." Mom clicks her tongue. "Babies are adorable. And if your Aunt Hannah ever left the house for something other than work, then maybe she could meet a man and have a baby of her own."

"Mom," I groan.

"I'm just saying." She points to the bag of shredded mozzarella. "Now tell us what happened while you dump that on top of here."

Picking it up by the corners — because I don't trust that they haven't grabbed it with their messy hands — I shake the rest of the cheese on top of the lasagna.

When I set the bag down, they're both staring at me again.

"You ready to tell us how you know this new owner?" Mom asks.

I puff out my cheeks. "He's just a guy I used to know back in college. I didn't realize he was in the industry, so I wasn't expecting to see him sitting in on the interview. It caught me off guard, is all." There, the truth without too much information.

"Guy from college?" Mom narrows her eyes.

Chelsea wiggles her eyebrows. "Did you date him? Is he like an ex-boyfriend or something?"

The tween is too clever for her own good.

Mom's eyes widen. "Hannah," she gasps. "Is it... you know... the football player?"

I let out a loud groan as I pinch the bridge of my nose.

way up the ranks at the company I now own. Meaning, for seven fucking years, she's been only twenty fucking minutes away. And I had no idea.

An ugly emotion twists around my heart.

What happened?

Why did she leave school, leave me, to come back to work at Petals? A place that — according to the dates on her résumé, she'd been working at since she was fifteen.

I click on the company's website, but it takes me to a disabled page. Going back to the map, I expand the information for Petals and see that it's closed.

It *doesn't matter*.

Back to the résumé, I stare at her schooling.

There's no mention of HOP U. No record at all of her time there. Like it didn't happen. Wasn't even real.

I shake my head at that thought.

It's her.

I know it's fucking her.

Same eyes. Same hair and freckles. Same vibrant spark of life.

I swallow, admitting to myself that she's not the same.

None of us are the same people we were in college.

For a long time — for too long — I thought about Hannah. I told myself I'd hear from her.

We never exchanged numbers during the week we knew each other, but she knew where I lived. She had to have. Everyone knew where I lived.

And even after that year, when I graduated and got drafted, she could've found me. It's not like my life was a secret. I was one of the highest-paid defensive tackles in the league. I've been on magazine covers. On talk shows and news shows and at celebrity events.

If she wanted to, she could have found me in seconds.

There were a few times over the years, a few nights when I was feeling especially lonely, that I'd search her name.

But she didn't have any social media, or at least none that I could find. And even though my buddy, Nate Waller, went into the tech business, I could never bring myself to ask him to look.

He would've done it if I asked. He knew how much her leaving fucked with my head.

But if he found her, and I know he could've found her, then what?

I just show up on her doorstep?

Beg her for answers?

What if she'd been married?

I stare at her name on the paper.

Still Utley.

Hopefully that means she's single. Or at least not married.

Just like I never got married.

It's not like I stayed celibate all these years. But I did make a point to only date women who didn't remind me of her.

Which, now that I think about it, probably saved me from marriage. Because no matter how much Hannah shredded my young heart by disappearing like that. A part of me always recognized that she was exactly the type of woman I'd want to spend my life with.

Not that any of that matters anymore.

Because when Hannah looked at me today, she looked at me like she didn't even know me.

EIGHT

HANNAH

"Good night," I call back to Mom and Chelsea.

They're going to stay up and watch another episode, or more likely three, of the new makeup artist reality show they found. It's entertaining, but unlike the two of them, I have an alarm going off in the morning.

Between the dining area and the kitchen is the staircase leading upstairs, but I take the short hallway next to it and head toward the back of the house.

My bedroom is the only one on the main level, across from one of the two bathrooms. The first and third generations of the family have bedrooms upstairs, sharing the other larger bathroom.

The floorboards, a light wood that is original to the house, creak beneath my feet.

I pass our little laundry room, and then on my left is the bathroom, and on the right is my bedroom.

It's a small room, but it's a corner room, so I have one window overlooking the side yard and one to the back yard, giving me lots of light when I happen to be home during the day and want to hide away with a book.

The space was actually meant to be a study, not a bedroom, so the entire wall that the door is on is covered with built-in bookshelves.

I step into my room and shut the door, and as always, it feels like I'm walking into my own personal library.

After pulling the curtains closed, I climb into bed.

As is customary, I brushed my teeth and changed into my sleep pants and tank top before the last episode. It's something Mom and I started doing back when I was in high school, so if we stayed up too late watching TV, we could go right to bed.

Small flickers of moonlight sift through the curtains, reminding me of a time I slept in a different library.

Pulling the blankets up to my chin, I close my eyes and let myself remember.

When we realized we'd been locked in, Maddox and I came together like magnets. Like there was no other outcome than us combining the way we did.

We used benches as a bed, and... *after*, I used his chest as a pillow, and we used his hoodie as a blanket.

I think about the paper football he had in his pocket, how he propped it against his chest and told me to make a wish and flick it onto a chair for the wish to come true.

I wished for Maddox to be the man that I marry.

And when the paper football went off course, he kicked it into place.

At the time, it felt like a sign. Like some sort of good omen.

But ever since then, I've decided it wasn't. That maybe his interference messed with our destinies. Like he rewrote our timelines with that one kick.

It's foolish, of course. Destinies aren't real.

My bed is unmade, how I left it, and I strip as I cross the room.

Naked, I walk into the attached bathroom and through to my walk-in closet.

After selecting a clean pair of boxers, I pull them on, then go back into the bathroom to brush my teeth.

The routine is second nature, and while I run through it, my mind wanders back to Hannah.

It stays on her as I spit my toothpaste into the sink.

It stays on her as I exit my bathroom and cross to my bed.

And I can't stop thinking about her as I pull the blankets into place.

With my arms spread out across the mattress, I think about that one night we had together. How I lay down just like this, on a bed made of benches, and how she curled up into my side. How her little hand looked on my chest, and how I could feel the warmth of her thigh as she hitched it up over mine.

I close my eyes and think about my Hannah Bunny.

How the first three times I saw her, she ran away. Like a scared little bunny.

And I think about her hiding today.

How she's still running from me. Acting like I'm a stranger.

But no matter how much time has passed, we're not strangers.

Maybe I need to remind her of who I am.

TEN

HANNAH

Crouched next to my chair, I pull open the bottom drawer of my desk.

Apparently, the companies were preparing for this merger for a lot longer than anyone told us, because the office upstairs is ready for us to start moving in on Monday. Hence me spending my Friday morning packing all my stuff.

Annoyance flares every time I think about it.

It's not like I would've quit just because Maddox was going to be the new owner. Well, truthfully, I might've. But now we'll never know. Because no one told us. But at the very least, I could have prepared myself better.

Never thought I'd think this, but thank god for Brandon. If he hadn't come into my office before my interview, I would've walked into that situation entirely blind.

I shove a handful of files into the box.

I didn't see any signs of Maddox yesterday, so I just need to get through the rest of today, then I can have the weekend to stew over my current predicament.

"Need a hand?"

The deep voice startles me, and I start to tip.

My arm jerks out in response, and I bang my elbow against the edge of the desk before losing my balance completely and ending up on my butt.

"Shit!" I grab my elbow with my opposite hand and rub at the pain as I sit on the floor.

"Hannah?" Maddox's voice moves closer until he's looking at me over the top of my desk.

Perfect. The exact man I was hoping to avoid today.

"You alright?" The large man takes a step around the side of the desk.

I stop rubbing my elbow to hold up my hand, palm out.

He takes one more step before halting. "Sorry. Didn't mean to startle you."

"You didn't." I don't know why I deny it. It's obvious he did. I'm on the floor, after all.

"Of course not." He presses his lips into a line, and I think the jerk is trying not to smile. "I forgot how accident prone you can be."

My mouth pops open, but before I can snap something at him, he bends down, hooks his hands under my arms, and lifts me to my feet.

A small sound croaks out of my throat as my heart stutters in my chest.

He shifts his hands so he's gripping my upper arms, steadying me.

His scent surrounds me as we stand chest to chest.

It's different than it used to be. Still soap and cologne, but more... grown up.

It's too much.

Being this close... having him reference our history... it's just all too much.

How dare he?

My nose starts to tingle.

I can't let him have this control over me again.

My cheeks start to burn.

"Hannah." His tone is gentle. And it's worse than the teasing.

I straighten my shoulders. "I don't know what you're referring to, Mr. Lovelace."

He narrows his eyes the tiniest bit as he takes a step back. But instead of just dropping his hands, he trails his fingers down the backs of my arms, ghosting them over my hurt elbow. "Sure you don't."

Goose bumps dance across my skin, but I ignore them. "Was there something you needed?"

Maddox crosses his arms over his massive chest, the fabric of his sleeves stretched tight over his biceps.

I don't want to notice how good he looks. But again, he's in a plain shirt and dark slacks, and he looks dangerously handsome.

I take a small step back.

He seems taller than he was in college, but maybe it's just that he stands with even more confidence.

Mad Dog Maddox was impressive in his twenties, but in his thirties, he's a force.

I cross my own arms, wanting to match his power pose.

My maroon and white striped shirt is buttoned all the way up, unlike Maddox's, and at my collar are two long strips of fabric I've tied into a bow. It's cute, but it's also a shirt I wear often, so no one will think I'm trying too hard to dress up on a casual Friday. Because I'm *not* wearing this for Maddox. I'm not trying to impress him at all. And if I have the loose-fitted shirt tucked into my snug but stretchy ankle jeans, that's because it's comfortable and has nothing to do with me thinking my butt looks good in these pants.

From where we are, I can see the restaurant is pretty busy, which makes sense since it's noon and downtown on a Friday. But the kid is already nodding.

"Yeah, we got a table ready." He waves a hand. "It was set up for a group coming in at twelve thirty, but we'll put them somewhere else."

I shrug. Sucks to be those guys. Then I angle my body to let everyone else go ahead of me.

"Pays to be famous." One of the guys, whose name I don't remember, grins at me as he follows the host into the restaurant.

Hannah rolls her eyes, but then she keeps them forward instead of looking up at me.

I take up the rear of the group as we make our way to the far side of the dining area.

Like all good sports bars, there's a lot of dark wood, hockey memorabilia on every wall, and a whole row of TVs above the bar — all playing hockey games or something sports related.

The host stops us at a rectangular table with four chairs on either of the long sides, and everyone starts to sit.

Hannah takes one of the end spots, and I swear Brandon lunges for the chair next to hers.

Casually, because I'm not a desperate man-child, I pull out the chair directly across from Hannah.

End spots give me more room for my wide shoulders. It's just a lucky coincidence that I'll be looking at my long-lost Hannah for the next hour.

TWELVE
HANNAH

This is a nightmare.

I've fallen asleep. I'm dreaming. And I'm having a nightmare.

I try to pinch my thigh through my jeans, but the material is too tight and I can't get a grip on anything.

Not that it would do me any good. I'm not lucky enough for this to be just a bad dream.

Right after we all sat down — me surrounded by the two men I want to see the least — the server came around to take our drink orders.

That gave me a whopping minute to try and compose myself.

Spoiler: it wasn't enough time.

Taking a slow, deep breath, I remind myself this is just lunch with some coworkers and our new boss.

I glance up at Maddox.

He's talking to one of the guys down the table about something football related, giving me a chance to take in his profile.

I hate it.

Because it's so perfect.

The trimmed facial hair. And the memory of the way it tickled the sensitive skin on my inner thighs.

The lips that are that perfect shade of pink. And the way they kissed me like I was all he needed.

Maddox places his elbow on the table, and I follow colorful tattoos down his forearm to his hand.

It's curled into a loose fist, but god, it's so big. If he flattened it out, it would take up the space of a dinner plate.

His fist loosens a little, and I have to tell myself to keep breathing. Because I'm remembering the way he looked, standing over me, naked in the shadowy library, stroking his length.

Maddox taps his pointer finger against the table, and my eyes snap up. Locking with his.

THIRTEEN
MADDOX

I move my attention back to the guy talking to me and bite down on my smile.

Getting under Hannah's defenses is going to be easier than I thought.

FOURTEEN
HANNAH

Heat crawls up my neck, and I busy myself looking at the menu.

Just chill, Hannah. Take a breath. And chill.

I was bound to see Maddox again. He's the owner of the company, and if today is any indication, he'll be at the office. Maybe not every day, since he wasn't in yesterday, but I gotta learn how to be normal around him.

I take another breath and make my eyes focus on the words in front of me.

It's fine.

This is all fine.

And if it becomes completely miserable seeing Maddox all the time, I can find a new job.

"And for you?" The friendly voice pulls my attention up, and I find the server at my side, beverages already set out on the table.

"Sorry," I apologize. The server has her little notepad in her hand, so I assume she's taking meal orders. "I'll have the..." I look down at the menu and read off the first thing I see. "The chicken Caesar wrap, please."

"Good choice. That's my favorite."

Her smile draws out my own, and I hand her my menu.

"And you?" She turns to Maddox.

His menu is already closed because, obviously, he's been paying attention. And while he hands it to the server, I lift my glass of Dr Pepper and take a sip.

"I'd like the ham and cheese sandwich, please," Maddox asks politely.

It takes me a second.

Just a second for it all to come crashing back.

And with the understanding comes the emotions.

Every emotion I've been trying to lock down since I heard his name on Wednesday. All the hurt and anger and betrayal that have been festering inside me for fifteen years. All of it snaps back into place like it never left.

My mouth is still full of Dr Pepper, and when I try to swallow it, my throat seizes.

I manage to get it down, but some of the bubbles hit wrong, making me cough.

I cough again, my eyes stinging as I set my cup down.

At my side, Brandon turns toward me. "Jeez, Hannah." He half laughs. "First time drinking?"

He lifts a hand like he's going to pat my back, but I don't want him touching me.

"Fine," I choke out, even as I fight not to burst into tears.

Why is Maddox toying with me like this? Is it not enough that he pretended like I didn't exist when I was at my most vulnerable? Can't he just keep doing that? Keep pretending our stupid fucking week together never happened?

"Hannah?" Maddox's voice is deeper than Brandon's, and it holds no humor.

"I'm fine," I repeat, not making eye contact with either of them.

I don't want anyone helping me. I don't need anyone to help me.

"Hate when it goes down the wrong pipe." Brandon chuckles at my side.

I clear my throat as gently as possible, needing the attention to move away from me. And thankfully Brandon turns back to his previous conversation.

I touch my fingers to the corners of my eyes.

Hold it together.

"Hannah." Maddox says my name quieter this time.

"I'll be right back," I say as I slip out of my chair.

I spotted the sign for the restrooms on the walk to the table, so I make a beeline for them now.

A tear drips from the corner of my eye.

Then a second follows.

I press my hand flat against the ladies' room door and push it open.

A woman is at the sink, but I keep my face tipped down and walk to the farthest stall so I can have my mental breakdown in private.

FIFTEEN
MADDOX

Guilt sits heavy in my stomach as I watch Hannah brush at her eyes while she hurries toward the bathrooms. Away from me.

I like ham and cheese sandwiches, but I'd be lying if I said I ordered that for any other reason than to get a rise out of Hannah.

But I figured I'd get a spark of indignation. Some sort of defiance.

I expected her to pretend like she didn't understand the reference. Or maybe for her to not remember at all.

I didn't expect to see her face fall the way it did. Didn't expect to see so much hurt fill her eyes.

I didn't mean to make her cry.

"You like ham and cheese?"

"Yeah." She eyes me like it's a trick question.

I hold one of the sandwiches out. "Here, I don't need all three."

"How'd you know I'd be on this floor?" Hannah looks around at our little corner of the university library. "And how'd you beat me?"

Satisfaction blooms in my chest. She's not running away from me this time. "Lucky guess. And athlete, remember?"

I see the moment she decides to give me a chance.

Hannah steps forward. And I smile.

So long ago, but I can still picture it like it just happened. I can still feel the way she made me feel.

I look at the empty seat across from me. How did she have such an impact on me?

"Don't worry about her. She's resilient," Brandon comments. And it makes me want to crush his wrist bones with my fist.

Because I know she is. She twisted her ankle, injured her nose, and almost fell off a step stool when I first met her. And not once did she ask for help. I had to pluck her from the air myself.

Brandon lifts a shoulder, like I asked him a question. "We've known each other a while now."

Known each other.

He's trying to make it sound like they're a couple. But I know they aren't. I can tell from Hannah's body language that she doesn't like him. Not like that.

Doesn't mean she didn't sleep with him in the past.

"Hmm" is all I respond with, because I'm pretty sure this prick is trying to gaslight me.

Another few minutes pass, and what started as guilt morphs into worry.

She's been gone too long.

I shift my legs, preparing to push my chair back, when Hannah appears in my line of sight.

She's so fucking pretty.

Her hair is up in a ponytail that sits high on the back of her head, and it allows me to see all of her beautiful face as she gets closer.

Hannah smiles at one of the servers she passes, but it doesn't reach her eyes.

But fake or not, she keeps the smile in place as she approaches.

Her cheeks are free of tears, and her makeup doesn't look smudged.

I glance at her purse as she hooks it to the back of her chair.

Did she fix her makeup?

Lowering herself into her chair, she flicks her eyes to me, and I see it.

Her mascara is perfect, her eyeliner is intact, but her eyes are bloodshot.

She's been crying.

That guilt expands.

I made Hannah cry.

But why the fuck does the mention of a sandwich make her cry?

I grit my teeth together.

This speculation is ridiculous. I just need to talk to her.

SIXTEEN

HANNAH

Settled in my chair, I can feel Maddox staring at me.

I want to ignore him, spend the rest of lunch looking anywhere else, but I force myself to meet his gaze.

His lips part like he might say something, but I mouth the word *don't*.

There is literally nothing he can say or ask me in this setting that would make my current mental situation better.

He shuts his jaw, and I have one second to stress over the fact that I just silently snapped at my new boss. But then my favorite server in the world shows up, distracting everyone with food.

All the side conversations cut off as the plates are set down.

The heartache half of me isn't hungry. But the half of me that's starting to feel more angry than hurt knows that not eating will only draw attention to myself.

After unrolling my silverware, I set the napkin on my lap and pick up my wrap.

By my second bite, Brandon starts posturing and asking Maddox questions about the solar industry.

And by my fifth bite, it's obvious to everyone, except maybe Brandon, that Maddox shouldn't be underestimated. He might be an asshole, but he's no one's fool.

Maddox picks up a fry from his plate, and I realize his fancy ham and cheese sandwich is already gone.

That first time we had food together, I teased him about how fast he ate.

I let my eyes lift to his, and he shrugs a shoulder, like he's acknowledging what I'm thinking.

It's another reminder of our past, but this one doesn't spear me in the heart like his food order did. This detail just feels... familiar.

As I finish my lunch, Brandon spends the next thirty minutes interrupting our coworkers to *show off* his own knowledge.

I'm embarrassed on Brandon's behalf, but the interrogation gives me a chance to put everything that happened earlier out of my brain.

Maddox's expression after he placed his order and I started coughing for my life didn't look fake. I don't think he meant to send me into a spiral. He just doesn't understand. He doesn't get it.

I'm trying to do us both a favor by pretending there's no history between us. I can't think of a single reason why he wouldn't do the same.

"Did you know the first solar panel was invented in 1883?"

Maddox gives Brandon the slowest blink I've ever seen before he replies in the driest voice. "You don't say."

A small laugh tries to break free, but I clear my throat to cover it.

Maddox narrows his eyes at me, but I pretend not to notice.

It's clear these two dislike each other, even if I don't under-

stand why. But Maddox is doing a better job of not looking like
a moron.

SEVENTEEN
MADDOX

As a group, we walk out of the restaurant and to the parking lot next door while the melted Gruyère and smoked ham sit like a rock in my stomach.

I want to tell Hannah to ride back to the office with me. Want to demand it, really. But singling her out now would put a spotlight on her. And even if I'm still a little bitter about her disappearing on me, I'm not looking to out our history in front of our colleagues. This issue between us is only between us.

I lift my hand in a wave as some of the guys call out their *goodbyes*.

I was planning to go back to the office. But maybe I won't.

"It's the BMW," Brandon says as he points to what must be his car.

It takes everything in me not to roll my eyes when he looks my way.

First, I would bet my left lung he made sure everyone knew he drove a BMW on the trip over here. No way this fucking tool didn't mention it a minimum of six times.

Second, is he seriously trying to show off to me? Money

doesn't mean shit. Not as far as someone's character is concerned. But I played pro ball. For a dozen years. A simple search online will tell you how much I made each year.

Hint: it was a lot. Like a fucking lot. And I was smart with it. Invested, saved, didn't buy multiple houses or blow money on boats or other dumb shit. So now, I have even more.

I nod to Brandon. "They make good cars."

I don't buy new cars every year. But I did buy one this year.

Stopping next to my vehicle, I try really hard not to smirk. Because I drive a BMW too. Or at least I drove mine today; this is hardly the only vehicle I own.

Brandon's car is more practical, with four doors versus my two. But costing approximately four times more than his, mine is more fun.

He does a double take, and I swear his lower lip thins.

I'd never shame someone for what they drive, but Brandon deserves a little humiliation.

Maybe we can arrange a company game of dodgeball, and I can chuck something at his face.

It'd make me feel better. And from the looks he was getting today, I don't think I'd be the only one aiming for him.

I imagine Hannah taking her own shot at him, and it almost makes me grin.

I climb into my car and wait while everyone splits between Brandon's car and the midsize SUV another guy drove over.

The SUV goes first, then Brandon, and then I pull out.

Traffic isn't too bad, so we stay in a row as we move down the street.

I decide I might as well head back with everyone else, so I continue to follow along.

The light ahead of us turns yellow, and the SUV goes through, but Brandon stops just as it turns red.

I drum my fingers on the wheel, pleasantly surprised he

didn't try to blow through the light. And glad because he has Hannah in there with him. If he put her in danger with reckless driving, I'd do more than embarrass him.

Leaning forward, I try to see Hannah through the back window. But she's in the front passenger seat, and she's short enough that her form is hidden by the seat and headrest.

The light turns green, and Brandon's car jerks forward. Clearly, he stomped on the gas.

"Fuckin —" I lift my foot off the brake as I start to curse the idiot, but then it happens.

A car crossing from the right is trying to run their red light at the same time Brandon is trying to jump the green. And they collide.

Hannah.

I slam on my brakes.

My heart beats painfully in my chest as I throw my car into park and scramble out.

I leave my door wide open as I sprint toward the two cars blocking the intersection.

Both vehicles are stopped. There's no smoke. No fire. But still, I feel like I can't breathe.

My shoes slap against the hard surface of the road.

Five more steps.

Three.

One.

I jerk on the passenger door handle, but it doesn't open.

Bending down, I look into Hannah's wide eyes through the window. "Open the door for me."

She nods, but the movement is frantic, and her lips start to tremble.

To my side, I hear someone get out of the other vehicle. It's gotta be the driver, but I don't pay them any attention.

shook me.

Next to me, Maddox moves his hand, holding it a few inches away from his side and turning his palm up.

He's offering his hand to me.

I feel another wave of tears build behind my eyes while I stare down at it.

I shouldn't take it.

I shouldn't allow myself to take any comfort from him.

There's no purpose.

The numbers don't add up.

There's no good outcome here.

But... maybe just for a moment.

I lift my hand and slide my palm against his.

Maddox doesn't stop his conversation with the officer as his fingers close around mine.

It's such a simple thing.

And yet, it feels like so much.

"Ma'am?" the officer says, like maybe he's said it before.

I blink up at the cop. "I'm sorry, what?"

"Just asking if you're alright. You were in the car too, correct?" he asks.

"Yeah, no, I'm okay." I lift my free hand in a lame wave. "Just kinda stunned."

The cop nods and goes back to talking with Maddox. I'm too distracted to listen. Too focused on Maddox's thumb as it slowly traces a circle on the back of my hand.

I'm totally fine.

I take a deep breath.

I don't need his help.

I exhale.

Okay, just one more minute of comfort.

Lifting my gaze past the bumpers, I see Brandon standing

in front of his car with his arms crossed, staring at Maddox. Or rather at our joined hands.

My fingers start to loosen their grip, not wanting to get caught, but Maddox tightens his hold on me.

When I look up at him, he's still talking to the cop, but he doesn't loosen his fingers.

"That you with the open door?" the cop asks.

I turn and see he's referring to Maddox's car, the driver's door sitting wide open as it idles in the lane.

"Yeah," Maddox confirms.

The cop makes an impressed noise. "I've got all the information I need to write up the incident. Both cars look drivable to me, so I'll have everyone clear out and contact their insurance companies."

"Sounds good." Maddox nods.

As the officer strides away, Brandon and our other two coworkers walk over to us.

"You guys alright?" Maddox asks the trio as a whole.

They all nod with sounds of agreement.

Maddox looks down at me and releases my hand, then sets his on my shoulder. "You feeling steadier now?"

Even though the summer day is nearly too warm, my hand feels cold without his holding it.

But the move is brilliant. Genius-level thinking. Because if I'd jerked my hand out of his, like I'd wanted to when I saw Brandon looking, it would have looked like an act of guilt. But now, well, now he just looks like a concerned boss. Maybe a little misogynistic by only checking on me, the one female. But to his credit, I was the only one acting like I needed help.

"I'm good." I look to the other three, trying to act normal. "Sorry. I sorta just..." I lift my shoulders, Maddox's hand still there. "Freaked out."

"Totally get it." One of the guys snickers. "Brandon's driving does that to me too."

"That wasn't my fault!" Brandon throws his hands up. "If that fucker —"

"Chill," the second guy laughs. "He's just messing with you."

"Whatever," Brandon grumbles. "The cop said we could go, so let's go."

Maddox keeps his hand on my shoulder. "Head back and get whatever you need from the office for the weekend, then head home. We'll call it an early day for everyone."

"Thanks, Boss Man." The first guy grins.

"Just trying to avoid any more excitement today. But take it easy, drink lots of water, and if any of you start to feel sore, go to the doctor." His hand slides across my shoulder to the top of my back, applying a small amount of pressure. "Alright?"

"Yeah. Okay." The two guys agree as Brandon scowls.

"Come on, Hannah." Brandon tips his head toward his car. "Let's go."

The thought of getting back into his vehicle makes my palms tingle.

"She's with me." Maddox's tone leaves no room for argument. And I have no intention of arguing. "I'd offer to take more, but my car only seats two."

Brandon's scowl deepens as the other guys turn their attention to Maddox's expensive-looking sports car.

"See ya at the office," I say before I let Maddox guide me toward his vehicle.

After two paces, his hand leaves my back as he steps away. But a moment later, he's back, handing me my purse.

"Oh, thanks." I take it, glad one of us remembered.

Maddox just hums a reply.

I know this is a bad idea — getting into a car with Maddox

Lovelace — but it feels like less of a bad idea than forcing myself back into Brandon's car.

Bright side of this whole mess? I can avoid ever having to ride with Brandon again. Since I'll just claim I'm still traumatized.

Go figure though. The one time I take Brandon up on his offer of lunch, simply to get away from Maddox, I end up in a car accident with the first and then riding alone with the second.

Maddox walks me to the passenger door and reaches past me to pull it open.

His car sits low to the ground, so I let my suddenly exhausted body fall into the seat.

"Buckle up," Maddox commands.

"Okay, Mom," I reply out of habit, even as I reach for the strap.

"Not your mom," Maddox growls before shutting my door.

Protected by the tinted windshield, I watch him as he walks around the front of his car.

He really is an incredible-looking man.

The height. The build. The way he holds himself.

Not my mom, indeed.

Maddox is Daddy material.

As he approaches his open door, I remember calling him Mr. Lovelace back in my office, and my cheeks start to heat.

I said it to be bratty. Because I wanted to snap at him. But as soon as it came out of my mouth, I remembered calling him that way back when. During our first ever kiss.

The car shifts as Maddox climbs into his seat, and I don't miss the grunt he lets out.

I almost open my mouth to say something. Ask if he's okay. Ask how his joints are holding up after a lifetime of tackling and being tackled. But I don't. It's none of my business.

His comfort was... nice. And appreciated. But I can't let myself get lost in it.

I can't let myself forget how easily he forgot me.

That thought alone is enough to put the first brick up in the walls around my heart.

Maddox was really decent to me just now. But he was also a real fucker before that.

NINETEEN
MADDOX

Brandon's car is already pulling away when I shift into drive.

The light is green, but I still move slowly, making sure to check the intersection before I cross through it.

Hannah is quiet at my side, face turned to look out her window.

My fingers twitch around the steering wheel.

I want to reach for her. Place my hand on her thigh or entwine our fingers again.

I want to feel her against me. Feel her hands pressing into my back, holding me close.

I want to erase the history between us. The doubts. The hurt feelings.

If we'd met now, our paths never crossing before this, I'd still want her. No fucking doubt about it.

But now is not the time to confront her about what she did fifteen years ago. She might not be shaking anymore, but the adrenaline crash will be hitting soon — if it hasn't already.

I clear my throat. "Do you need anything from your office?"

"Hmm?" Hannah finally turns her head to look at me.

TWENTY-ONE
MADDOX

This fucking minx.

I watch her disappear between a row of cars, ducking her head like it will make her invisible.

"Alright, Hannah." I press my hand down on my aching cock. "It's gonna be like that."

With the sudden urge to laugh, I take my foot off the brake and roll forward.

TWENTY-TWO
HANNAH

Crouched in front of a car that isn't mine, waiting for Maddox to leave because my car is parked on the opposite side of the level, I curse my hussy of a vagina.

The engine sounds get quieter, and when I peek over the car, I see Maddox is gone.

Standing, I straighten my clothes and pretend I'm not turned on.

TWENTY-THREE
HANNAH

It's been weird spending the week adjusting to my new office while also spending every night applying for new jobs.

But it's for the best. A must.

Even if I don't see Maddox every day, the stress of it all has me constantly on edge.

Is today the day he'll just walk into my office again?

Will he be in the break room when I go get my lunch out of the fridge?

Is he going to be inside the elevator when the doors slide open?

It's seriously too much. I've started keeping TUMS at my desk because I swear I'm going to start having indigestion.

I glance at the clock and see it's already a few minutes after five.

One person, then two, then another one, walk past my door.

With my projects for the week complete and nothing left to do to delay, I shake a few orange Tic Tacs into my palm. And when I put them in my mouth, I don't think at all about my kiss with Maddox. He won't ruin these like he's ruined everything else.

It's been exactly one week since I tucked and rolled out of Maddox's car, and since then, I've seen him twice. The first time was from across the break room when he walked in to get coffee as I was putting my lunch in the fridge. Thankfully, another employee was standing by the mugs, and he greeted Maddox, giving me the distraction to slip out. The second time was when I was walking to the ladies' room. Maddox was coming from a different direction, possibly going to the men's room, which was located next to my destination. I lengthened my stride to beat him there and then spent longer than necessary sitting in one of the stalls to ensure we wouldn't exit at the same time.

I can't live like this.

I follow up my Tic Tacs with a TUMS.

Another cluster of coworkers walks past, and I know I can't delay anymore.

Standing, I straighten my skirt.

No one said we had to dress up for the party, but I decided to wear my favorite pleated skirt. It's olive green and stops just past my knees, but it has a slit up one side to about midthigh. So it's still work appropriate but isn't too matronly.

And if I wore my best bra and my scoop-neck off-white short-sleeved shirt with it, it's just because they pair well.

Same for shoes. The wedge heel might be a bit high, but the faux leather matches my shirt perfectly. So it's not trying too hard; it's just coordinating.

But by the time I step through my door, my pinched toes remind me why I don't wear these shoes to work.

"Hey, Hannah."

I lift my hand and join the two project managers heading toward the elevators.

rapher set up in front of it, and written in large letters across
the clear material are the words MinneSolar and MVP and
Dream Team.

When two people step inside the box, the imagery comes
together.

It looks like a magazine cover.

"Clever, isn't it?" Maddox's voice sounds from
behind me.

I nod, not wanting to talk to him, and thankfully, the two
project managers jump into conversation with him about where
he got it made.

"Hey, thanks for the car service." One of the ladies beams
at Maddox. "It's a great idea."

I glance up to see him dip his chin. "You're welcome. I've
used them in the past, and it's worked out well. What's the
point in having an open bar if no one can drink?"

"Hear! Hear!" Someone raises their beer as they walk
past us.

A few days ago, we all got an email with a sign-up sheet for
free rides to and from work for anyone who wanted to have a
drink tonight, and twenty dollars for anyone not drinking who
preferred to drive themselves to and from the office. I don't plan
on getting drunk, but a few free drinks on Maddox's dime was
too tempting to turn down.

We shuffle ahead, and the ladies turn around to place their
orders with the bartender.

"What's your poison?" With the other women's attentions
occupied, I know Maddox is asking me.

"I usually end up with wine." I try to keep my tone casual,
as though the last time I saw him, he wasn't kissing my damn
face off. "You?"

"Wine is good." There's a gleam in his eye I don't know
what to do with. "I'm partial to whiskey though."

The women ahead of me move to the side, and it's my turn to order.

The counter behind the bar is lined with liquor bottles, cans of beer, and a trio of wine bottles, displaying the options. I can't read the label on the wine bottles from here, so I just ask for a glass of white.

"And for you, sir?" the bartender asks, causing Maddox to step up next to me.

"A glass of Perro Rabioso on the rocks, please."

The bartender grins. "Makes sense."

I watch him pour my glass first — into a real wine glass — then he picks up a bottle of brown liquid with an angry-looking dog on the front.

And then it hits me.

"That's yours, isn't it?" I tip my head to look at Maddox.

The side of his mouth pulls up as he takes both drinks from the bartender and holds the wine out for me. "Yeah, it's mine."

I wrap my fingers around the stem, and he gently clinks our glasses together.

I don't have a response for him, so I lift my glass and take a sip.

"Good?" he asks.

I take another sip. "It's alright."

It's divine.

Maddox chuckles, but thankfully, someone steps up in line behind us and says his name.

Using the chance, I slip away.

I bite down on my urge to laugh. She's right. I did do that.

"Mr. Lovelace, this is my wife." Roberts beams next to the kind-looking woman. "Wife, allow me to introduce you to our new owner, Maddox 'Mad Dog' Lovelace."

From the edge of my vision, I can see Hannah shake her head.

"Mrs. Roberts." I hold out my hand. "It's a pleasure. And please, it's just Maddox."

Mrs. Roberts places one hand in mine while pressing the other to her chest. "Hi! We're huge fans. Or we were. Well, we still are."

I let go of her hand. "I appreciate that."

"And this party." She waves her hands around. "It's so nice. Oh!" She turns and picks up a couple of glasses off the table behind her. "Hannah dear, here's your wine."

Hannah takes it as Mrs. Roberts hands the other drink to her husband.

"Thank you," Hannah says as she smiles at Mrs. Roberts.

I want her smiles.

Something niggles inside my ribs.

I want more than her smiles.

Mrs. Roberts is still looking at Hannah. "Gosh, you know who you'd be perfect for? Our nephew." She nudges her husband. "Wouldn't they be perfect together?"

I take back every nice thought I just had about the woman.

"You're right!" Roberts replies, his bushy eyebrows jumping up his forehead.

I consider demoting him.

Hannah shifts next to me, and I expect her to nicely turn them down.

"You think so?" she asks. "What's he like?"

Slowly, I turn my head to look down at her.

Mrs. Roberts claps her hands. "Oh, he's so sweet. Are you single?"

"Sure am." Hannah takes a long sip of her wine as Mrs. Roberts makes more sounds of excitement.

"He's an accountant too," Mrs. Roberts explains. "Works for his dad, my brother, who's..." She giggles. "Also an accountant."

Gee, what a fun fucking family.

"And he likes football!" Roberts chimes in. "I know you're a big fan, so maybe you could watch a game together or something."

I keep my eyes on Hannah. "You like football?"

She glances up at me for just a second, then shrugs her shoulders.

Roberts laughs. "This girl can talk ball with the best of them. Pretty sure we did an after-game report for all your games during our lunch breaks. Or, well, your games until you retired."

"You don't say?"

Roberts nods, then turns back to Hannah. "Our nephew has a nice big TV too. Perfect for game nights."

So my little Hannah Bunny watched all my games, did she?

"Do you have a picture?" Hannah asks, and I have to bite the inside of my cheek to stop myself from growling at her.

She doesn't want some little accountant twerp.

She wants someone... bigger.

While Mr. Roberts leans over the phone with Mrs. Roberts's, looking through photos, I angle myself toward Hannah, keeping my voice low. "What are you doing?"

She blinks up at me. "It's hard to find a good man nowadays. It's this or sifting through the dick pics in my inbox."

An angry sound rumbles out of my chest. "Men are sending you dick pics?"

"Online dating is tough." She tries to smirk, but it's more of a cringe.

My hands ball into fists. "You will not —"

"Here he is." Mrs. Roberts thrusts her phone forward.

I stare at the man on the screen and can't stop myself from asking, "How old is he?"

"Twenty-six." Mrs. Roberts beams.

Hannah clears her throat. "He's cute."

She's a fucking liar.

He's not cute. He looks like a goddamn baby. Because he is a baby. Hannah doesn't need someone a damn decade younger than her. She needs someone one year older.

A server appears at my side with a glass on his tray. "Bartender said to bring this over."

I already had the one drink I was allowing myself tonight, but this conversation requires more liquor.

"Thank you." I take the glass, then raise it and my gaze to the bartender across the room.

He gives me a thumbs-up.

Taking a long sip, I make a mental note to double the tip I was planning to give the staff.

TWENTY-FIVE

HANNAH

As enjoyable as it is to push Maddox's buttons, I need to get out of here.

Tipping my glass back, I finish off what's left of my wine. "It was so nice to meet you," I tell Mrs. Roberts. "But I need to be heading out."

She shakes my hand, then pulls me in for a hug.

Roberts is grinning at his wife's behavior but still gives me a hearty handshake. "See you Monday."

"See you Monday." I step back and spare a quick look up at Maddox. I don't care if I'm rude to him, but I don't want to appear rude in front of other people. "Bye, Maddox."

I turn away too quickly for him to respond and make a beeline for the elevators.

I'm half tempted to swing by the dessert table again, but I've already had three mini cheesecakes, and any delay is a chance I'll get stuck talking to Maddox again.

About half the people are still here, living it up, and there's no one else waiting to leave.

Standing alone, I press the button for the elevator and shift my weight in my stupid shoes.

The wine has helped me forget how sore my poor little toes are, but I'm still more than ready to kick these shoes into the back of my closet.

A ding alerts me to the elevator door opening, and I step into the empty cab.

Remembering I need to get my purse, I press the number for our office floor.

As the doors slide shut, I lift my gaze to get one last look at the party, relieved that no one is looking or heading this way.

The doors are three inches from closing when a large hand sticks itself into the opening.

The doors slide back open, and Maddox steps into the elevator.

TWENTY-SIX
MADDOX

I turn to face the party, staying silent as the doors close, cutting us off from everyone else.

TWENTY-SEVEN
HANNAH

He hasn't said anything. Hasn't reached for me. Hasn't moved a muscle. But my heart has started racing, and my chest feels heavy with each breath.

Carefully, so I don't draw his attention, I reach my hand out and press my fingertips to the wall, bracing myself.

The elevator comes to a stop on our floor, and Maddox doesn't move.

My hands start to tremble. Not from fear, but from something else.

When another long second passes without him moving, I step forward. Maybe he's not getting off here. Maybe he's just waiting for me to exit, then he'll press the selection for the parking levels.

His wide frame is half blocking the door, so I have to shift sideways to get out. And I give him my back as I shuffle past.

Something brushes against my ass, and I take my next step quicker.

Just get to my office. Get my purse. And go.

Footsteps follow me off the elevator.

They follow me down the hall.

All the way to my door.

I turn the handle, push my office door open, and step inside.

I don't turn around, but I hear Maddox follow me.

I hear him shut the door.

And I hear him lock it.

I stop beside my desk, facing the windows that look out into the city. They're tinted like upstairs, so we can see out, but no one can see in.

There's a footstep, then another.

"What are you doing?" I whisper.

Maddox steps closer until the front of his body presses against my back. "I'm reminding you."

"Of what?"

Hands settle on my hips. "Of the type of man you need." Warm breath ghosts against my neck. "The type of man you crave."

I try not to arch my back. I try really hard. But when he flexes his fingers against my soft flesh, I cave.

"We shouldn't." I try to reason — with him, with myself.

"We shouldn't." He pulls me flush against his body, letting me feel how ready he is. "But we're going to."

And fuck if that isn't the truth.

"Turn to me," Maddox demands against my ear.

He's putting it on me.

Making me be the one to do it.

I reach down and place my hands over his.

It would be so easy to push his hands away. To *not* turn around.

So easy.

But fucking impossible.

I twist, turning to him.

TWENTY-NINE

HANNAH

Rough hands turn me around, shoving me until I'm bent over my desk.

My bare breasts press into the cool wood surface, and I'm lost to it.

To the overwhelming desire roaring through my veins.

I can still taste the whiskey that coated his tongue.

Can still feel the tug in my nipples from where he was sucking them.

Maddox yanks my skirt up, exposing my bare ass, the thong I decided to wear today covering nothing.

"Fuck." He grips my ass in his big hands and spreads me, making himself groan again.

He hooks a finger around the material covering my pussy and pulls it aside.

I know I'm wet. Soaking. And he hasn't even touched my clit yet.

I tilt my hips, exposing myself to him even more.

A blunt tip rubs along my slit.

"So fucking wet for me." Maddox presses a palm to the center of my back, holding me in place.

I ball my hands into fists.

"You have to be quiet, Hannah." The tip of his cock nudges my entrance. "Can you do that?"

"Yes." I nod.

"Prove it." Maddox thrusts forward.

His entire — almost too big — length fills me, and my mouth opens to scream.

But the air evaporates from my lungs, and I can't make a sound.

My pussy seizes around the intrusion, and my body can't decide if it's suffering from pain or pleasure.

Maddox moans. And it isn't quiet. It vibrates through me.

He pulls out, almost all the way, then pushes back in.

I arch.

It's been so long since I've been fucked.

He slides mostly out, then slams back forward.

Hell, maybe I've never actually been fucked, because this is...

He rocks his hips, and I whimper.

"It's too much." I try to shift away from him, even as my hips tilt to take him farther.

Maddox leans forward, pinning me in place with his body. "It's not too much."

He rolls his hips again, pushing himself even deeper.

"It's too big," I cry.

"No, Babe." He nuzzles against my neck. "It's just right."

He doesn't stop moving. His cock keeps sliding in and out of my channel. He keeps stretching me.

"You were fucking made for me," he growls against my ear. "You were built to take all of me."

He reaches a hand between my hips and the desk.

The underwear I'm still wearing is pulled tight across my clit. And every thrust causes friction that brings me closer to the edge.

Maddox tugs the material aside. "You're gonna come for me." His fingers rub circles. "I'm gonna play with this sweet little clit, and you're going to come all over my fucking dick."

It's hard to breathe.

Hard to think.

Hard to remember why this is the worst idea ever.

Maddox starts to move faster, his hips snapping forward, bouncing me against the desk.

His own breathing is getting loud.

Maddox pinches my clit between his fingers, squeezing, rubbing.

Small sounds I can't stop start to crawl out of my throat.

"That's my girl." Maddox moans, his mouth against my shoulder. "Even better than I fucking remember."

He shoves his hips forward — hard — hitting a spot even deeper than before. And there's no going back.

His fingers pick up speed.

He rocks into me.

His heavy breath echoes in my ear.

It's too much.

I flatten my hands on the desk and push at it. "It's too much," I choke out.

"It's just right." Maddox presses into me harder.

And I implode.

A strangled sound gets trapped in my lungs, and my body convulses under his touch.

"That's it. That's it. Come for me," he chants as his thrusts become jerky. "That's my Hannah." His fingers don't stop. "Keep coming. Clamp that pussy down on my dick, Babe."

My muscles tighten. My core pulses, and his cock does the same.

Maddox groans, and I can feel his cock throbbing as warmth fills me.

THIRTY

MADDOX

I shudder as the final drops of my release fill Hannah's fluttering pussy.

"Jesus." I press a kiss to the side of her neck, then start to pull back.

Keeping my cock inside her, I straighten up so I can look down at where we're joined.

I burn it into my memory — the sight of her skirt rucked up and my dick buried in her heat.

Thinking about the fact that we could've been doing this for the last fifteen years makes me want to spank her ass.

Next time.

After sliding free from her warmth, I slip her underwear back into place.

When I step back, Hannah pushes up from the desk and adjusts her bra and shirt back into place.

When she's standing and facing me, she shifts her hips and makes a face.

I smirk, knowing my cum is leaking out of her, making a

mess of her panties. And soon enough, it's going to be coating the inside of her thighs.

"I know it's uncomfortable, but it's the least you owe me," I joke, attempting to put the bad blood behind us because I want to do that again.

Hannah's shoulders sag. "Owe you?"

I stare back at her. "I was kidding. But yeah. Owe me. Fifteen years' worth, actually."

She shoves at my chest, and I take a step backward, not expecting it.

Hannah moves to her desk and retrieves her purse from one of the drawers.

"What?" I ask, not understanding this hot and cold shit.

She slams the drawer shut and tries to glare daggers at me. But they don't land the way they're supposed to because her eyes are filling with tears.

"You're the one who didn't call!" Her voice cracks. "At least I tried."

THIRTY-ONE
HANNAH

I push past Maddox and fling the door open.

I don't even care if I run into anyone. I'm sure I look like a mess. But I can't spend one more second in his presence.

Tightness fills my chest.

The least you owe me.

I hug my purse to my chest.

Never again.

Never again will I be fooled by this man.

All those years ago, in that cursed library, I thought of him as the big bad wolf.

In my mind, it was a joke.

But it's true.

Only this isn't a fairy tale.

And no one is coming to save me.

THIRTY-TWO
MADDOX

Stunned, I watch her disappear.

I drag a hand down my face.

What the fuck is she even talking about, saying I *didn't call?* We never exchanged fucking numbers. There was no way for me to fucking call, even if I wanted to.

I clench my jaw. How did I go from what was possibly the best fuck of my life to standing here feeling like complete shit?

Done with this day, I pull out my phone and transfer the money for the tip to the catering company. The party will wrap up in thirty, and I don't need to be there for it.

I storm out of Hannah's office and make it a few steps before I notice Brandon walking down the hallway toward me.

He looks past me, probably to Hannah's door, but I just nod at him as I pass.

What we do is none of his fucking business.

THIRTY-THREE
HANNAH

The hired car slows to a stop in front of my house.

"Here we are, ma'am." The driver makes to unbuckle himself like he's going to come around and open my door.

"Please, don't get out of the car." I undo my seat belt and start to open my purse to give him a tip.

He holds up a hand. "No need for extras. Mr. Lovelace took care of it."

Of course he did.

Of course he's a generous tipper.

Of course everyone fucking loves him.

I give the driver a tight smile and climb out.

My feet throb with every step, but the pain has nothing on the ache between my thighs.

Or the one in my chest.

After *what happened* in my office, I got off on a random floor on my way down to the lobby. I didn't allow myself to break down because there wasn't time for that, but I did clean myself up as best I could.

The inside of my nose starts to tingle as I climb the steps to my house.

Not. Yet.

Not yet. Not yet. Not yet.

Putting a blank expression on my face, I open the front door.

Mom and Chelsea are in the living room, with an open pizza box on the coffee table.

"She's home!" Mom calls, like I've been gone for days, not just *the day*.

"How was the party?" Chelsea asks, looking away from the TV screen.

"Fun," I reply, then make a show of prying my shoes off. "But remind me never to wear these again."

"I'll take them."

Mom snorts at Chelsea's excitement. "Pretty sure it'll be three years before your feet are big enough to wear Hannah's shoes."

"That's about how long it'll be before I'm willing to wear them again." I wiggle my toes and sigh.

"The price of conventional beauty standards is often pain." Mom repeats a phrase we've all heard before. She's not wrong. "Did you eat? There are a few slices of Hawaiian left."

I place my hand on my stomach. "The food at the party was actually pretty good, and I ate plenty. I'm gonna go take a shower and give the toes a little pampering, then I'll come back out and veg with you guys."

"Sounds like a good plan." Mom lifts her mug, which I know is filled with peppermint tea.

I head down my little hallway and into my bedroom to grab my comfiest pair of sweatpants and my softest T-shirt. Then I cross the hall to my bathroom.

I don't let myself think about Maddox as I strip.

I don't let myself think about what we did as I pull back the shower curtain.

I don't let myself remember how eager I was, how much I wanted to please him, as I turn the water on.

I don't let myself think about how good he felt as I open the music app on my phone and select my shower playlist.

But when I set my phone on the edge of the sink and step into the shower, and the noise of music and running water fills the room, then I remember.

Lowering myself to sit in the tub, I remember the way Maddox called me his Little Bunny.

I remember the way heat filled my belly when he called me his good girl.

I remember the feeling of his hand on my throat. The control he took. The relief I felt giving it to him.

I remember wanting to let the past go. Wanting to take what he was offering.

But then I remember what he said.

It's the least you owe me.

I remember the way I felt hollow as soon as he said that.

I remember how the stickiness between my thighs suddenly felt dirty.

I remember feeling cold.

And that's when the tears start.

They mix with the streams of water running over my body, disappearing as soon as they fall.

Maddox was so intense, the way he touched me, the way he commanded me.

And he was just as serious when he said that. The heat of desire was gone, and he was left staring at me like I was the one who'd wronged him.

I press the heels of my palms into my eyes and try to rub the vision of him from my brain.

But it doesn't work. And it doesn't stop the tears.

Tears of frustration. Tears of anger. Tears of self-pity.

It wasn't my fault my mom had a stroke.

It wasn't my fault we couldn't afford to live if someone wasn't running the shop.

Wasn't my fault life is so disgustingly unfair.

A hiccuped sob gets locked in my lungs.

It wasn't my fault he never fucking called.

Owe me.

I never really expected him to show up one day and save me.

Never truly thought he would.

But it didn't stop me from dreaming, from hoping for a different outcome.

For a happily ever after. For some light in the dark.

For someone to choose me.

I tip my head down.

I hoped for something that would never happen.

And now, all these years later, I can admit that after we kissed, after that day when he hugged me in the middle of the street... I hoped all over again.

I believed in something that didn't deserve to be believed in.

But this time, there's no one to blame but myself.

And it makes me so goddamn angry.

Opening my mouth, I let out the most forceful silent scream I can manage.

I ball my hands into fists, and I lean into it.

I suck in another full breath and let it out again.

I pretend he's in front of me, and I pretend I'm screaming loud enough to shatter the windows around us.

I pretend I have a different past.

I pretend I never met Maddox.

Picturing it, a week at HOP U, having never met Maddox, the pressure inside me finally pops, and I sag forward.

Another tear gets washed away down the drain as a thin layer of sadness settles over my jagged pieces, dulling the pain. Because I don't want that either. I don't want to lose those good memories.

I just need to find a way to keep those memories in the past. Because in the present, there's no more thinking about Maddox Lovelace.

No more hoping for translucent dreams.

No more thinking with my vagina.

No more.

Reaching down, I massage my feet before I finally get up and finish my shower.

With towel-dried hair, I enter the living room.

Chelsea has a movie up on the screen, ready to play.

Mom is in her chair, and Chelsea is sprawled across the couch, so I take my usual spot in the creaky leather chair that's so old it looks like it came from the side of the road but is actually perfectly molded to my butt.

The movie starts, and I prop my feet up on the footrest.

We don't watch movies together every weekend, but we do it often enough that I've used it as an excuse not to date.

I look over at my niece.

The older she gets, the more she looks like her mom. And the more I'm reminded just how fragile life is.

How fragile everything is.

And it's the perfect reminder of why I can't get caught up in Maddox and lose my job.

Silently, I take a long, slow breath.

If I really think about it, taking emotions out of the equation, it doesn't matter that Maddox never called. It never would have worked anyway.

I couldn't go back to HOP U. I had to work full time — more than full time — at Petals. And even if he wanted to try a long-distance relationship, we never would've seen each other. Between his football schedule and my working and taking care of Mom, there was no time.

And then Maddox moved across the country and became a professional football player, becoming more and more famous as each year passed.

My heart squeezes.

And while he was doing that, my life changed again. Because my cousin passed away, and then Chelsea came to live with us.

I was twenty-five, supporting my mom, and suddenly, we had custody of a child.

It was ten years ago, but I still remember that day like it just happened. The call that Chelsea's mom had passed away unexpectedly. And the news that she left her two-year-old daughter in our care, guardianship split between me and my mom.

My cousin was smart doing it that way. My mom wasn't in a position to take full-time care of a toddler. And neither was I.

I cried so much that first week.

Feeling anguish over losing the cousin I loved. Feeling terror over being in charge of a child's life. Feeling selfish for not wanting the responsibility. Feeling the crushing weight of knowing I had no choice, and that I wouldn't want it any other way.

Chelsea was too young to remember her mother, but we made sure to tell her stories and show her pictures as she grew up. I was always Aunt Hannah, and Mom was always Grandma to her.

And so, for the past decade, it's been us. The rest of the family is gone, either from old age or from freak illness or accidents.

The family curse.

A sad smile pulls across my lips.

Chelsea started calling it that. And sometimes it does feel like a curse. Like we're doomed to only have one another.

But that's more than some people have. And I'd choose these two over anyone else.

"What are you thinking about?" Chelsea's question has me raising my eyes.

"Hmm?"

"You're smiling weird."

"Oh, just thinking about... popcorn." I lie, not wanting to tell her I'm thinking about the curse.

"Sure." She rolls her eyes.

"I'd take some popcorn," Mom chimes in, lifting her eyes to the clock on the wall. "And it's my birthday in two hours, so I feel like someone else should make it."

Chelsea quickly puts her finger to her nose, the universal sign for *not it*.

Making a scene of sighing loudly, I push out of my chair and head to the kitchen.

While the bag expands with popping noises in the microwave, I open the laptop I left on the counter and click through the tabs that I still have open, checking the status of each job application I submitted this week.

THIRTY-FOUR
MADDOX

Sweat beads across my forehead, and I close my eyes, focusing on the strain in my thighs.

Pretty eyes stare up at me.

I squeeze my eyes tighter, trying not to picture Hannah as blood pumps through my veins.

I thrust up, grunting with the motion.

I open my eyes and stare at my reflection as I step forward and rack the bar into place.

My music is blaring through the speakers of my home gym, the basement walls reverberating around me. But it's still not enough to drown out the memory of Hannah's voice.

I tried.

More than anything else, those two words have been on repeat in my brain.

I grab my towel off my shelf and swipe it across my face.

What the hell was she talking about?

What had she tried to do?

I press the towel over my closed eyes.

I'm missing something. I have to be.

The music cuts off as my phone starts to ring.

I snatch it off the shelf and look at the ID.

I almost don't answer it, not in the mood to shoot the shit. But then I remember the favor I asked for.

"Waller," I say as soon as the line connects. "You finally pull that background on Petals?"

He lets out an awkward chuckle that has my senses tingling.

"What?"

"Well." He chuckles again. "It's one of those *isn't it funny* sorta things."

"What the hell are you talking about?" I'm being a dick, but I'm starting to get a bad feeling about whatever he's called to tell me.

"Well, I got a little sidetracked with some other stuff this week and forgot all about that flower shop you wanted me to look into. But then I happened across the name today, Petals, and it reminded me."

"And how did you come across the name?"

He pauses a beat. "On an application."

My spine stiffens. "What sort of application?"

"And it's *funny*" — he ignores my question — "because I'd been looking at the name on the résumé, thinking to myself, *Why does she sound familiar?*" That bad feeling solidifies. "And then I read through her work history, and saw she worked for Petals, and thought *Huh, what a coincidence...*"

"Are you telling me Hannah has applied to work for you?" I grit out through clenched teeth.

"That's exactly what I'm telling you. Now, are you going to tell me what the fuck is going on?"

"Nothing is going on." I start to pace.

"Nothing is going on." Waller repeats my sentence using his *dumb* voice. "Sure. Except my best friend is keeping fucking secrets from me."

I heave out a breath. "I'm not keeping secrets. I asked you to look into Petals, didn't I?"

Waller scoffs. "Yeah, but you failed to mention it had anything to do with Hannah Fucking Utley. Shit, man, it's the girl who fucked up your head our senior year."

"She didn't —" I start to argue.

"She also happens to be applying at my company." He talks over me. "And I can clearly see on her résumé that she currently works for *your* fucking company. So, sure, tell me again how nothing is going on."

"Fuck off," I sigh. "I don't need to add your bullshit friend guilt to my plate right now." I spin and head back the way I came. "And you're not hiring her."

"No shit, man. I'm not going to hire someone my bestie hates."

I stop pacing. "I don't hate her."

"No?" He sounds more curious than surprised.

"No. And don't use the word bestie. We're not twelve-year-old girls."

Waller makes a humming sound. "So you don't hate her, but you're still trying to blackball her?"

"What?" I shake my head. "No, that's not — I'm not trying to prevent her from getting a job. I... Fuck." I drop down to sit on the weight bench. "I didn't know she applied for other jobs." The knowledge of it finally sinks in, making me feel sick. "I don't want her to leave."

"So..." Waller drags it out. "Was it a surprise when you found out she worked for you? Or..."

I roll my eyes. "I didn't buy that company to get close to Hannah. I had no idea she even worked there."

Though, had I known, I might've.

Waller whistles. "Bet that was a slap to the nuts."

I grimace. "Basically."

"And..."

"And what?"

"And what?" He mocks me. "You just said you had no idea she worked for the company you bought. You really think I'm not gonna want to know more?"

"That was the hope," I say dryly.

"Well, hope in one hand, shit in the other." He uses our old coach's favorite phrase.

"As you can imagine, it didn't go great." Then I think about it and almost laugh. "She pretended not to know me."

"Chick ghosts you, turns up a decade and a half later, ghosts you again — to your face — and you think it's funny?"

I shake my head. "Talking to you is worse than talking to my mother."

"Keep it up, and I'll add her to this phone call. Don't test me."

"God, you're a pushy bitch." I stand back up and start pacing again. "I didn't know she was there until she came in for one of those new company interviews we did."

"Fuck." I can picture the wince in Waller's voice. "That must've been a moment."

"Yeah, well..." I feel like a dick admitting this part, but I know Waller will understand. "The interviews were boring as hell, and I had some emails from my lawyers about some contracts that I needed to go through. So I was doing emails on my phone the first, like, half of her interview." I blow out a breath, wondering how I hadn't recognized her voice. "I didn't even look up until someone said her last name, and by then, she had plenty of time to get over any of her own shock."

"So when you finally paid attention, she was already locked down."

"Basically."

"But you go into the office, right? So you've seen her?"

"Yeah."

"And have you confronted her about her little disappearing act?"

"Kinda. No. Fuck, I don't know." I turn and walk back across the gym. "She's giving me all sorts of mixed signals. Giving me the evil eye one second, crying over a ham and cheese the next. But then last night after... I said something, and she snapped at me about not calling her. But that doesn't make sense because we never exchanged numbers."

I tried.

The heavy weight of doubt latches itself on to my shoulders.

"I think I'm missing something," I admit.

It's quiet on the line for a long moment.

"You still there?" I ask into the phone.

"I'm here. Just busy wondering how you've already managed to sleep with this woman without, it seems, actually talking to her."

I stare forward at the wall. "I hate you."

Waller laughs. "No you don't. But for real, maybe quit thinking with your dick for an entire minute and go ask her — straight out — what the hell happened."

"I do hate you," I mutter.

"Nah, you just hate that I'm right. Now, do you want to know what I found out about Petals, or would you rather wait and ask her about it?"

I groan. "You word it that way so I'm the jackass if I ask you to tell me." I can picture his shrug. "But I've been on my back foot this whole time, and I'm tired of not knowing what's going on. So tell me."

"The business belonged to Ruth Utley. She started it about forty years ago with a Theodore Utley — found a marriage certificate, so they were Mr. and Mrs. But a few years later, it shifted to be just in her name. I looked because I was curious if it was a divorce thing, but instead of divorce papers, I found a death certificate."

"Hannah's dad?" Emotion slams into my throat.

"Yeah. If my math is right, she was just a baby."

"Shit."

"But the Mrs. did a good job with the business. It was pretty successful. Not enough to get rich off, but enough to raise a kid on. There's really not much to tell after that, so I jumped ahead to when it closed. It lines up with when Hannah went to the solar industry."

"I don't get it."

"What don't you get? Her take-home pay now is better than what she was making off that store."

"But that's what I mean. It wasn't her store. Maybe her family owned it, but if she had to basically run the place, why leave for college in the first place?" I shake my head. "Something had to have happened. I need to go talk to her."

"Let me put the phone down so I can do a slow clap for you."

"This is why I don't tell you things." I stride out of the gym and go up the stairs two at a time until I get to the main level.

Waller chuckles, then sighs. "Look, I won't call her back about this application. But if she randomly applied for the open accountant position at my company, I can promise you she applied for more."

"I know." I'm sure she did. She probably applied for a dozen other jobs.

"Welp, I'm not exactly sure what you want, but... good luck."

I hang up the phone, knowing exactly what I want.

I want to know what happened.

And I want Hannah.

Now I just need to figure out if she still wants me too.

THIRTY-FIVE
HANNAH

"Stick them in the fridge," I tell Chelsea as I hurry out of the kitchen toward the front door.

It's Mom's birthday today, and we just finished making cinnamon rolls to bake after dinner, and our Chinese food delivery is early.

They knock a second time on the front door.

"Coming!" I call out, wiping my hands on the apron I'm wearing over my shorts and a T-shirt.

I snag the cash tip off the bench where I left it and pull the door open. "Here —"

My body freezes at the sight of Maddox.

He's standing right there.

On my front step.

I swing the door shut, not wanting to talk to him after last night.

Right before the door closes, Maddox puts his palm out, stopping it.

I know if I pushed on it, he'd drop his hand, let me close the door in his face.

But he's here.

I pull the door back open.

I watch him watching me.

"I'd like to talk to you." His tone is so sincere it makes my teeth ache.

"Maddox —"

"Come on, bring the food in!" Mom calls from inside the house.

I eye Maddox, and I call back over my shoulder. "It's not the food."

"What is it?" Mom shouts back.

"It's a man," I say flatly. And it almost looks like the edge of Maddox's mouth twitches.

"Well, shut the door in his face or let him in, but quit letting all the cold air out."

This time, I'm certain his mouth twitches before he leans over me into the doorway. "Evening, Mrs. Utley."

He calls it out in his sweetest voice, so I'm not even surprised at my mom's reply.

"Bring him in!"

"Mom," I heave out, exasperated.

"It's my birthday, Hannah." She says it like it's a reason to invite the male species into our home when she doesn't even know who's at the door.

I look up at Maddox.

He puts his palms up. "It is her birthday."

I bite down on my lip.

There is no good outcome to this.

"Why are you here?"

Maddox takes a step closer. "Because I want to talk to you."

I keep staring at him. "You're not going to fire me, are you? Because I don't think that's an appropriate thing to do at my house."

He rears back. "Fire you?" He shakes his head. "No. That's not — that's ridiculous. I just want to talk to you, and I don't want to do it at work."

"And you have my home address...?"

"It was printed on your résumé. I didn't even have to steal it."

I bite my lip some more. "My phone number was also on there."

He nods.

"You could've called," I point out.

"Wasn't sure you'd answer my call."

His call.

God, what a mind fuck it would be to have him call me now, after all this time.

We're staring at each other when Chelsea comes up to stand beside me. "Who's this guy?"

Maddox glances at Chelsea, then slowly lowers his gaze back down for a double take.

THIRTY-SIX
MADDOX

I stare down at the little girl. Her eyes... they're just like Hannah's. Same shape. Same light brown color.

But her hair... It's dark.

Like mine.

I look back at Hannah.

She's watching me with her arms crossed over her chest.

I glance back down at the girl.

"Is..." I swallow as a strange mixture of emotions coats my skin. "Is she mine?"

Hannah and the child blink at me.

Could it really be?

Do I have a kid?

"Seriously?" Hannah says the same time the kid says, "Ew."

Ew?

What the hell does —

My jaw clenches.

Did Hannah have another man's baby?

The girl rolls her eyes at me, then looks up at the adult

beside her. "Aunt Hannah, did you seriously sleep with this guy?"

"Chelsea!" Hannah sounds like she's trying to chastise the kid but also like she's trying not to laugh.

Wait.

"Aunt?" I question.

"Close the door!" Hannah's mom shouts again as the kid disappears into the house.

Pinching the bridge of her nose, Hannah steps back. "Might as well come inside."

THIRTY-SEVEN
HANNAH

Maddox steps past me into the house.

I can't believe this idiot thought Chelsea was his kid.

Or that I'd keep a child hidden from their father.

Idiot.

Maddox pauses at the bench to toe off the tennis shoes he's wearing, leaving him in white socks, worn jeans, and a gray T-shirt that shows off more of his tattoos than I've ever seen.

I untie the apron I have on and pretend we aren't wearing matching outfits. With my jeans in the form of shorts and my T-shirt a white V-neck.

Normally, I don't feel comfortable wearing shorts around anyone other than my family. But I remind myself that Maddox saw a lot more than my thighs last night.

I shut the door harder than necessary.

Don't think about last night.

But as I watch his back muscles bunch under his cotton shirt, I can't help but think about it. He's just...

I pull the apron over my head.

It doesn't matter if he's sex incarnate.
Never again.

THIRTY-EIGHT
MADDOX

I should probably feel bad about crashing Hannah's mom's birthday party. But I also have a feeling that without her mom's insistence, I'd still be standing outside.

The small entryway opens into the main room, with a living room — jam-packed with furniture — on my right and a dining room on the left.

A bouquet of flowers sits in the center of the round table, and a pair of balloons is tied to the back of one of the chairs.

The house is probably a century old, with scuffed wood floors and archways between every room, making it feel small. But it's cozy.

The floral-patterned rugs and curtains don't exactly strike me as Hannah's taste, but I never even saw her dorm room, so I can't really claim to know her style.

A woman, who must be Hannah's mom, walks into the dining room from what I'm guessing is the kitchen on the far side of the room.

She's the same height as Hannah, with similar honeyed hair, only hers is mostly gray.

"Hi, Mrs. Utley. I'm Maddox Lovelace."

The woman stops midstride, and her eyes widen. "Mad Dog?"

My smile is genuine. She's not exactly my usual fan demographic. "That's me."

I hold out my hand, and she moves closer to take it. "So nice to meet you, dearie. Hannah used to talk about you all the time."

"Mom!" Hannah snaps from somewhere behind me.

We both ignore her as I grin. "Oh really?"

Mrs. Utley smiles up at me, letting my hand go. "Made me watch all your games with her."

"Mom." Hannah tries for a sterner tone.

"Really?" I glance over my shoulder at a scowling Hannah.

"Really." Her mom agrees. Then she leans around me to look at Hannah. "Oh hush. Young love is nothing to be ashamed of."

Hannah groans as my brows raise.

She talked to her mom about me? About love?

I probably shouldn't preen over that information, because if Hannah talked about me, I'm sure she said some bad things too.

"Call me Ruth."

"It's a pleasure to meet you, Ruth. Happy birthday."

"That's sweet of you." She reaches up to pat me on the arm. Then she does it again, giving my bicep a squeeze. "I thought you retired."

"Jesus Christ," Hannah mumbles behind me.

I lift both arms, flexing for my crush's mom.

"Okay." Hannah reaches up and pulls one of my arms down. "That's enough." She tugs on my wrist, turning me to face her. "Let's go talk so you can be on your way."

"You two can talk after dinner," Ruth answers for me.

I came here with feelings of guilt and hurt and confusion

twined around my neck, hoping for a heart-to-heart conversation where we could clear the air about what really happened fifteen years ago. So I should be on my best behavior, playing nice and doing whatever Hannah asks of me.

But teasing her is just too much fun.

"Yeah, Hannah." I grin down at the pretty woman staring at me with fire in her eyes. "It can wait until after dinner."

"Good." Ruth spins on her heel. "I'll grab another place setting."

Hannah and I watch each other as her mom retreats.

"Maddox." She says my name quietly.

"Bunny," I respond at the same level.

She purses her lips and balls her hands into fists. "If you're just here to fuck with me —"

"No." I cut her off. "I came to talk. And potentially apologize."

She watches me, looking all over my face for tells. And she must see something that makes her believe me.

Her shoulders drop as the tension around her releases, and she rolls her eyes. "*Potentially*. You're such a jerk."

There is zero heat behind her insult.

"I promise I won't do or say anything to make this dinner weird." I hold up a hand like I'm swearing an oath.

She narrows her eyes. "Doubtful."

There's a knock at the door.

Hannah starts to turn, but I step past her. "I'll get it."

I study the kid. "What's the curse?"

She shrugs. "Nothing big. Just that everyone who loves us dies."

I think my mouth drops open.

The fuck did she just say?

A pea flies through the air and bounces off Chelsea's cheek. "No talk of curses on my birthday. Birthdays are immune."

Chelsea wipes her napkin across her cheek, then goes back to eating.

I clear my throat and turn my head to look at Hannah.

Everyone who loves us dies.

Jesus fucking Christ.

Hannah's lips are pressed together. She's definitely trying not to laugh.

How the hell is that funny?

Hannah dips another wonton into the container of sweet-and-sour sauce, casual as ever.

I think about the house.

The curtains framing the window. The many pairs of kid-sized shoes at the front door. The abundance of comfortable furniture in the living room behind me.

These three live here together.

I'd bet my savings on it.

Because everyone who loves us dies.

Something desolate settles in my stomach next to the sesame chicken.

Hannah reaches over and pats my forearm, probably trying to snap me out of my mental spiral. "Don't worry, Maddox, you can't catch it from proximity."

I swallow through the tightness building in my throat. "You sure about that?"

Hannah nods. "It's one of the rules."

Ruth huffs. "Since when have you cared about the rules?"

When I met Hannah, I thought she was a bit of a Goody Two-Shoes. But I'm starting to think that's not true.

Maybe it's her quick comebacks that started to change my mind. Or maybe it was fucking her over her desk last night during the employee party that gave me the hint.

"And who did I learn that behavior from?" Hannah looks at her mom.

"No idea what you're talking about." Ruth takes another bite of her food.

"Plus," Hannah tells the table, "we're not getting married. We're not even dating." She holds up a hand. "I mean, we won't date. We can't. Not that we would. But even if we wanted to, he's my boss." She points her finger between us. "And we don't want to."

Everyone stares at Hannah.

She's adorable when she's flustered.

"Well, technically." I lift an egg roll to punctuate my point. "I'm not your boss. I just own the company."

FORTY-ONE
HANNAH

Maddox sits back in his chair with a groan, and I don't know if it's from eating that second cinnamon roll or from losing the last round of poker to Chelsea.

We don't actually play for anything, just bragging rights, but I don't think Maddox has lost at cards to a twelve-year-old before.

"I concede defeat." Maddox lifts his hands.

"How gracious of you." Chelsea snickers as she stacks her chips.

Tonight has been... nice.

Surprisingly nice.

Devastatingly nice.

Maddox came here *to talk*.

Talking could mean a lot of things, but no matter which way this conversation goes, I don't expect I'll enjoy it.

"Welp, I think it's time for some reality TV therapy." Mom pushes her chair back from the table. "We'll clean up later. You two" — she points to me and Maddox — "can go talk in Hannah's room."

"If I have a boy over, will you let us talk in my room?" Chelsea asks as she heads toward the couch.

Mom follows her. "Of course. When you're thirty-five."

Maddox and I watch each other, his amused look to my slightly pained one.

"Shall we?" He pushes up to stand.

I don't miss the way he grimaces getting out of the unforgiving wood chair.

"How are your knees?" I ask before I can think better of it.

But even if I hadn't been outed by Mom and Roberts over the last twenty-four hours, it's no secret that playing pro football damages your body.

He shrugs. "I'm nearing thirty-seven and have the knees of a sixty-five-year-old. So they're doing great."

I shake my head and gesture for him to follow. "Come on, old man. Let's go talk."

FORTY-TWO
MADDOX

We cut across the house to the back of the living room, but instead of heading up the stairs, Hannah leads me down a little hallway.

She hesitates for a second, then walks through an open door.

Following, I find myself in Hannah Utley's bedroom.

It's small. Probably the same size as my walk-in closet. But it's comfortable.

I glance at what must be a full-size mattress and try not to imagine how much I would not fit on that bed.

The built-in bookshelves make me think this may have been designed as a study, but Hannah has turned it into a nice bedroom.

"I don't have any chairs in here." She stops at the head of the bed and turns to face me. "But we can sit on the bed if you'd like."

My eyes roam over the neatly made bedding.

I want to feel it. The cream-colored comforter. The mattress. All of it.

But I don't sit. I want to stay standing for this.

I focus my attention on the woman in front of me.

There's no great way to lead into this, so I just start. "Last night, you said *you're the one who didn't call.*" She rolls her lips together as she watches me. "But we never shared our numbers, and I know you know that. So I need you to help me understand."

Her eyes close. "I shouldn't have said anything. It doesn't matter."

"It does matter," I tell her.

She opens her eyes, and they're full of sadness. "Why?" Her tone sounds so defeated.

So I tell her the truth. "Because I missed you."

FORTY-THREE
HANNAH

My throat constricts.
Because I missed you.

FORTY-FOUR
MADDOX

I take a step closer as I watch her fight to keep her features even. "Since seeing you again, I've thought about it a lot. And all I keep coming up with is that there's something I'm not understanding. Something I don't know." I want to touch her, but I keep my hands at my sides. "What happened, Little Bunny? What made you run?"

She pushes her hands into the front pockets of her shorts. "I wasn't running. Maddox..." Hannah presses her lips together. "Do we really need to do this? Can't we just pretend...?"

"No pretending." Now that I'm here, there's no stopping. "Just the truth."

Hannah nods once. "My mom... Right after, when I got back to my dorm room that morning." She refers to our night in the library. "I got a call from a nurse. My mom had a stroke."

"Fuck," I breathe out.

"She was in the hospital."

"Jesus, Hannah."

"I had no choice. I had to come home."

I think about the way our hands parted when we left the

"This — some girl. She said she overheard you telling people you were transferring back home."

I shake my head. "I never told anyone, Maddox. I sent an email to my boss, but I never said the words out loud to anyone. You were basically the only person on campus who knew I existed."

And he didn't even look for me.

Fuck, this all hurts as much today as it did back then.

FORTY-SIX
MADDOX

"Please leave." She's back to not meeting my eyes. "Now. Please."

I shift my weight, starting to step forward.

I don't want to go.

I don't want to leave her, looking like I just broke her heart all over again.

But she's asking me to leave.

"Alright." I step back.

I'll do what she asks now, but this conversation isn't over.

I turn and take the two strides to the door.

When I pull it open, my gaze is drawn to the bookshelf right next to my shoulder.

And there, on the shelf in Hannah's bedroom, is a book with a label taped to the spine showing that it's property of the HOP U Library.

The book.

My copy of *The Count of Monte Cristo* that went missing after our night together.

The one she read to me, with my chin resting on her shoulder and her voice filling my mind.

I step out of Hannah's room and into the hallway.

All these years, and she kept the book.

FORTY-SEVEN
HANNAH

I sink onto my bed, confused and sad.

For so many years, I wanted to have this conversation with Maddox, but now that it's done, I don't actually feel any better.

"I tore it up." Essie's tone holds no apology. "I did you a favor and tore it up before you could ruin your career over some nerdy —"

I hang up on her.

I hang up because I can't listen to another second of that bitch's voice.

Setting my phone on the passenger seat so I don't smash it to bits, I close my eyes.

I'm such a fucking asshole.

Essie is an asshole too. A completely shitty human to do what she did.

But I believed her.

I believed some woman I didn't even like and lost the one I was starting to love.

Self-loathing fills me.

Hannah left because her mom almost died.

She left because she had to take care of her and run the family business.

She left, waiting for me to call.

I said something foolish about how much our time had meant to me.

I press my hands against my chest.

If I'd known, I could've told her how much she meant to me too.

I could've been something good in her life.

I could've helped her. Come down on my free weekends. Visited after the season ended.

But I didn't.

I stayed at school.

I did everything I could to forget her. All because of Essie. Essie...

I shove my door open and gulp in fresh air.

After Essie told me Hannah left, I turned around and went

right back into the house. I went up to my bedroom and locked myself in. And after that, at every party, at every turn, Essie was there. Always flirting and touching. And I always rebuffed her. Always told her I wasn't interested.

Except for that one night.

It was a bad loss. I had some bruised ribs. I drank too much. And when she followed me upstairs, I didn't push her away.

I barely remember it. Only remember that I was feeling majorly sorry for myself and that she was the opposite of Hannah.

But even then, even when I thought Hannah had left me without a word, I still regretted it.

I told her to leave as soon as we woke up, and I never touched her again.

That morning was the most disgusted I've ever been with myself.

Until now.

I squeeze my eyes tighter, picturing Hannah from tonight. Her smiling eyes at dinner. The way she joked with her niece and her mom. The way she snapped a towel at me when I tried to enter the kitchen to help with the cinnamon rolls.

She's happy.

She's surrounded by family that loves her.

Everyone who loves us dies.

I press my fist harder against my chest, over my racing heart.

She found happiness, but I don't think it was easy.

I try to just breathe.

The least of what you owe me.

I force my eyes open, looking out at the night sky.

I finally got my Hannah back, finally got to feel her warmth again, finally got her to let go with me. And that's what I said to her.

What you owe me.
God, I'm such a piece of shit.
Pulling my driver's door shut, I shift the car back into drive.

FORTY-NINE
HANNAH

"Good night." I usher Mom toward the stairs.

Ever since I came out of my room, I could tell she wanted to talk to me about Maddox. But having him here for dinner is one thing. Talking about our history in front of Chelsea is another.

"Good night," Chelsea calls down from the top of the steps.

Before Mom can stall, I flick off the lights in the living room.

"Yes, yes, good night to everyone," Mom huffs, then continues upstairs, accepting that I don't want to talk tonight.

It's not that late, but we've done nothing but indulge in good food all day, and I think we're all equally ready to lie in bed and scroll on our phones.

I double-check the front door, then the back, making sure they're locked, then head into my room and shut the door.

Already in my pajamas — another loose tank top with a thin pair of sleep pants — I leave my light off and drop onto my bed.

I cried a little after Maddox left. But unlike the other times, it was more from an overall feeling of depression rather than piercing heartache.

I believe him about the letter.

There's no reason for him to lie.

But it's all just so... disappointing.

The lost time.

Ships passing in the night.

So close to...

I sigh.

So close to what?

Even if he'd gotten the letter and called, it wouldn't have meant anything.

One year later, he'd have gone to play with the pros, and I couldn't have followed. Even if things were good between us, I couldn't have asked him to financially support my mom so I could go with him to Arizona.

I almost roll my eyes because, after watching those two all night, I actually don't doubt that Maddox would've helped in any way he could.

But we weren't his responsibility.

In the dark, I turn my head toward my bookshelves.

I noticed his pause when he was leaving, and I know he saw it. *His* book.

I always felt a little bad about keeping it since it was library property. But I weighed the book's importance to me against the weight keeping it would have on my cosmic karmic scale and decided it was worth it. I'd take the hit to keep a part of him close to me.

My eyes stay focused on the spot as I think about that night when I read the beginning to Maddox.

I climb out of bed and turn on the small lamp on my bedside table.

In the dim light, I go to the bookshelf and trail my fingers down the spine before I pull it free.

I've read this book cover to cover so many times that the binding doesn't so much as creak when I open it.

The pages fall open to the first line.

On February twenty-fourth...

Something taps against my bedroom window, startling me, and I drop the book.

It lands on the top of my foot, sending a zing of pain up my leg.

"Shit!" I lift my foot in the air and shake it around.

There's another tap. "Hannah?"

I freeze. "Maddox?" I thought the noise was a branch.

I pick up the book and slide it back into place before limping to the window.

The fact that we can hear each other so well is more proof that we need to install new windows in this house. The drafty things are practically worthless.

Grabbing the edge of the curtain, I pull it aside.

Standing on the other side of my window, moonlight casting his features in shadows, is Maddox.

"What the hell are you doing?" I don't whisper, but I keep my voice low.

"I..." He runs one of his big hands over his head. "Can I come in?"

I look at him and then at my narrow window frame. "Not through the window." Biting my lip, I tip my head toward the front of the house. "Go to the door."

He gives me one serious nod, then steps back through the oversized bushes lining the house.

I don't know what he's doing here. And even though I'm the one who told him to leave not much more than an hour ago, seeing him lifts some of that depressive feeling.

I hurry through the house and am nearing the front when I remember that my tits are on full display in this shirt.

I pause but decide not to care.

He's the one who came to my window when all the lights in the house are off. He shouldn't be expecting a bra.

I pull open the front door as he mounts the steps in a single stride.

Maddox opens his mouth, but I lift my finger to my lips, and he snaps his jaw shut with a nod.

Stepping back, I hold the door open, then close and lock it once he's inside.

He's in the same clothes he was in before. And he slips his shoes off in the same spot.

I cut past him and lead the way back to my bedroom.

His steps are quieter than usual behind me, like he's making a point to step lightly.

This man.

I don't know what he's here to tell me, but the fact that he couldn't wait even one night to do it does something to the defenses inside me.

He follows me into my bedroom and gently closes the door behind us.

Not wanting to stand again, I climb onto my bed and sit cross-legged at the top of the mattress, gesturing for him to sit at the foot.

He keeps one foot on the ground, and his other leg is bent on the mattress in front of him.

Maddox makes a face. "Hold on."

He stands back up and moves around to the other side of the bed, sitting in the same position, only this time, his other leg is bent on the mattress.

I raise a brow. "Everything okay?"

"Knees." He shrugs. Then he looks at me for a long moment before saying, "I'm sorry."

"Maddox —"

He shakes his head. "I made a call."

"Tonight?" I don't hide my surprise.

"Yeah."

I grab one of the pillows from behind me and hug it on my lap. Both to cover my nipples that are poking through my shirt and for comfort. "Who did you call?"

He holds my gaze. "The woman who told me you left."

The bitter, jealous person inside me shakes her fist at him. "You talk to her often?"

"No. Never."

"Then how...?"

"I remembered her name and figured she followed me on social media. I was right." I almost snort at his cockiness, but since he was right, I guess I have nothing to laugh at. "But we..." He trails off, and I don't really need him to finish that sentence.

"So you found her?" I prompt.

"I messaged her asking for her number, and she sent it immediately." He makes a face. "Even though I'm pretty sure she's married with kids now."

"That's nice," I say with heavy sarcasm.

His shoulders rise and fall with a big breath. "She was always a jersey chaser. I should've fucking known." He shakes his head at himself. "I was so stupid for not putting it together when it happened."

"You're not stupid, Maddox."

His expression is pained. "She saw you leave the letter. And she read it." The thought of someone other than Maddox reading that letter has me squeezing my pillow tighter. "Then she ripped it up so I'd never know."

"And pretended like she overheard me so you wouldn't go looking," I finish, seeing it all so easily.

Maddox hunches forward. "I can't believe I believed her."

"Maddox, it's easy to believe her when it was the truth."

"No. No, don't make excuses for me. She *happened to find me* when I was on my way to the library. She set me up, and I fucking fell for it. I didn't even go to see if she was telling me the truth. I just believed it and went back home." His fingers open and close around the comforter.

I hate this.

I hate that this is what happened.

That everything between us was undone so easily.

But I also hate seeing Maddox like this.

I reach out and place my hand on top of his knee. "It was Saturday. Even if you had gone that day, no one working would've known where I was. I'm pretty sure my boss didn't even check her email on weekends."

"I should have gone." Maddox tightens his fists around the material, not listening to me.

"There's no —"

"I didn't go back to the library for a long time. When I never saw you again on campus, I knew you were gone. But at the end of the school year, I just couldn't let it go. So I went to the library every day for two weeks, hoping to see that one friend of yours."

"Friend?" I furrow my brows.

"The short one."

"Sissy?" She was the nice coworker who befriended me during my short time working there.

He makes a sound. "I never knew her name, but I thought maybe she'd know where you were. But she wasn't there."

"I think she transferred out after the first semester. I still talk to her sometimes. She lives here. Works at some fancy gym

I bet you'd like." I try to lighten the mood, but his face is tipped down so I can't see his expression.

I've been so mad at Maddox for so much of my life. It's good to know what happened, to finally put it all together, but truly, I just don't want to be mad anymore.

"I slept with her," he blurts out.

"Sissy?" I ask with a laugh, since I've met her wife.

But Maddox shakes his head, not lifting it. "The girl who lied."

"Oh." I grimace.

He finally looks up, guilt covering his features. "I'm sorry. It was only one —"

I lightly squeeze his knee. "Maddox, I did not expect you to be celibate. You don't owe me an explanation."

Yes, I hate the fact that he slept with the skank who caused so much pain. But it was half a lifetime ago. And even if he believed a lie, he's just as much a victim in this as I am. I don't blame him.

Maddox watches me, rolling his lips together. "Can I hug you for a while?"

"A while?" My mouth pulls into a small smile.

Maddox nods, then stands.

I expect him to circle around the bed toward me, but he pulls back the covers and climbs in, jeans and all.

"What are you doing?" I snicker.

"Come here." He lies on his side facing me, then starts to pull me to him.

"Okay, okay." I slap his hands away so I can slide under the covers.

I shift so I'm facing him, and he pulls me into him, with an arm around my waist, until my face is against his chest and his chin is resting against the top of my head.

One of my hands is tucked between us, trapped between his body and mine, but I drape my other arm up over his side.

We shouldn't be doing this.

I still work for his company; none of that has changed.

He tightens his arms around me. "I know you said I don't owe you an explanation, but I... I was pissed after a loss and got drunk, and she was the opposite of you," he rattles out.

The opposite of you.

I sigh. "Maddox."

"No, I just —"

This man isn't going to listen.

I tip my head back so I can look up at him. "The first guy I slept with after you was a skinny blond man about my height."

Maddox palms the back of my head and presses my face back into his chest. "I don't want to know."

I tilt my head to the side. "Then the next guy."

"I get it." He turns my face back into his chest. "Less is better." His body expands with a breath.

I feel a little better, knowing it bothers him too.

I tip my head back to the side so I can admit it out loud. "Because they were the opposite of you."

I kiss the top of her head.

Then I press my nose into her hair and inhale her scent.

It's soft and floral and all Hannah.

Her body relaxes into mine. "This isn't what I expected when you asked for a hug."

I tighten my arms around her. "I told you it would take a while."

"Mm-hmm." Hannah relaxes even more.

"I'm so sorry," I whisper.

"You didn't know," she mumbles back.

"I should have tried harder." I slide my palm up and down her spine. "What can I do to earn your forgiveness?"

"You're already doing it." She curls her fingers against my side. "And I'm sorry too. I knew where you were — everyone did. But I thought you wouldn't want to hear from me."

And just like that, Hannah drifts off into sleep while I hold her, flayed open by her last comment.

We only spent one week together. Tuesday through Saturday. That was it. But that week left an impact on both of us.

We were both hurt by the other.

And we both tried to forget.

Hannah knew how to find me, but she didn't reach out because she thought I'd reject her. And I could've hired someone to find her but didn't because I thought she'd abandoned me.

We both made assumptions, and they were all wrong.

And because of that, we lost so much time.

I hug her tighter against me.

Despite everything, being with her still feels so easy.

We fit. The perfect equation.

I felt it all those years ago, and I made the mistake of not telling her.

I won't make that mistake again.

FIFTY-ONE
HANNAH

The mattress shifts beneath me.

There's a creak and then a thud as something large falls to the ground.

I blink. "Maddox?"

"Tiny-ass bed," he grumbles from below the edge of the mattress.

I bite my lip to keep from laughing. "You okay?"

"Fine." He places a palm on the mattress and pushes himself up.

When he starts to climb back into bed, I shake my head. The lamp is still on, but I can tell the room is lighter than it was.

"You need to go. I don't want Chelsea seeing you here." Then I do laugh. "I can't believe you thought she was yours."

Standing, Maddox puts his hands on his hips and stretches out his back. "Well, can you blame me?"

"She's only twelve." I snort. "If she was yours, I would've had like an..." I give up on the math. "Eighteen-month pregnancy." I shudder.

He hums, then asks, "When did she come to live with you?"

"It was just before she turned two. Her mom, my cousin, passed away from an infection, and her dad was never in the picture, so she was left in our custody."

"And your dad," Maddox asks, meeting me next to my bedroom door.

My lips pull into a soft smile. "Really want to get all the details squared away, huh?"

Maddox nods.

"My dad died when I was one. Fell and hit his head, and it all went perfectly wrong. I don't remember him, but Mom still has photos of him around the house, so I feel like I do."

"That fucking sucks, I'm sorry."

"The curse sucks."

Maddox gives a slow shake of his head. "This is one of those *laugh or cry* things, isn't it?"

"A classic case." I smile.

Of course, I'd love it if my dad and cousin were still around, but you can't change the past.

"So, it's just the three of you, then?" he asks.

"Yep. Just us girls."

"Seems like you and your mom did right by your cousin." Maddox dips his chin. "Chelsea is a good kid."

His words fill me with familial pride. "Thank you."

Stepping past him, I reach for the door handle.

"Do you want more?"

I pause and turn back to face him. "More...?"

"Kids," he clarifies.

Kids. He says it just like that. Like it's a perfectly reasonable question. Like we've been dating for years and are considering marriage, and it's time to talk about kids.

And then I register what he didn't say.

It was just *Do you want more?* End of question. Not *Do you want more of your own* or *Do you want to have your own kids.*

Affection for Maddox rocks through me.

I've always been Aunt Hannah to Chelsea. She's always been my niece. It's who we are to each other. But she's mine, just like I'm hers. And I don't need her to call me mom in order to feel like the parental figure I know I am.

I wet my lips and decide that the truth is the best answer. "Honestly, I don't think I do. I already have the perfect child in my life. And her life is only going to get busier, so it's not like she'll suddenly need me any less. Plus, I got to skip the *no sleep infant* stuff while experiencing everything else. So, I think I'm good."

The side of his mouth pulls up. "I think you're good too."

"What about you?" I ask quietly, needing the answer even though I'm a little afraid of what it might be.

His mouth stays in that half smile. "Never really felt comfortable around little babies. But I seem to have a thing for hot aunts."

FIFTY-TWO
MADDOX

Standing here, looking at Hannah, I feel more at peace than I have in a long time.

It's that feeling you get when you think you lost something important, and so much time has passed that you figured you'd never have it again, but then you find it. You dig through some drawer you haven't used in years, and there it is. And the memory hits you with a familiar comfort.

"I want to kiss you," I tell Hannah, needing her to know.

Her eyes lower to my lips.

But when I lean down, she presses her palms into my chest. "Maddox..."

"Yeah, Bunny?" I keep my voice low.

"We shouldn't."

It's a lie.

We absolutely should.

But I'll let her have her win in this moment.

"Alright." I stand up straight, and it takes Hannah a long second before she lowers her hands from my chest. "Walk me out."

I savor the way her fingertips trace a trail down my stomach before she lets her hands fall completely away and turns to the door.

I didn't miss the way her tits look in that fucking shirt. The way the material is clinging to the swells of her breasts. Or the way her damn nipples are still begging for attention.

But I was here for serious reasons, so I kept my eyes on her face, even though it killed me.

Now, as I follow Hannah through the house, I don't bother being subtle as I stare at her ass, watching her hips move with each step.

And then there's knowing about the sweetness that lives between her thighs.

It's been just over twenty-four hours since I had my hands on her pussy. But it's been fifteen years since I had my mouth on her there, and we need to change that soon.

Hannah slows, reaching the front door.

I slide my feet into my unlaced tennis shoes and step through the doorway, stopping on the other side of the threshold and turning to face Hannah.

Dawn is breaking behind me, covering her features in the softest glow. And her eyes...

She looks the way I feel.

"Maddox," she whispers. "I want to kiss you."

I lean down, just a little. "We should."

Hannah shifts onto her toes, and I bend the rest of the way to meet her.

Our lips connect with a gentle brush, feeling like not enough and yet the perfect amount.

I lift my hand and gently circle my fingers around the front of her neck.

Her skin is so soft and warm beneath my calloused palm.

The perfect smooth to my rough.

I want to deepen the kiss.

Want to hold her tighter.

My body is ready for more. But I'm not positive Hannah's is.

Not yet.

I slide my hand off her neck and pull my mouth back from hers.

Hannah's cheeks are flushed, and her chest rises with quick breaths.

"Good night, Utley."

She glances past me toward the sunrise. "Morning, Lovelace."

I take a step back. "Lock your door."

"I know how to take care of myself," she tells me, one hand on the door.

"I know you do, Babe. But let me do some of that caring too."

FIFTY-THREE
HANNAH

I shut and lock the door, then watch through the peephole as Maddox walks to his car.

Let me do some of that caring too.

My forehead drops to the door.

Being with him — around him — it's just so goddamn easy.

It shouldn't be. Not after all this time.

I let my anger toward him cloud my happiness for so long.

It felt like it was a part of me. That bitterness. And I thought I'd have it forever.

But it's gone.

Just like that, it's gone.

I don't want to be angry anymore. I don't want to be hurt.

I don't want to put caution before passion.

I don't want any of that.

I just want Maddox.

FIFTY-FOUR
MADDOX

I'm lingering.

I know I am, and it's starting to feel obvious, but I want to see her. And I don't want to do it by barging into her office first thing on a Monday morning.

There's no reason I can't change the company rules and lift the no-fraternizing policy, but I'm almost certain Hannah wouldn't like that. And the last thing I want to do is make her uncomfortable at work.

I add another packet of sugar to my coffee mug and stir it with the same spoon I've been using for the last ten minutes.

As certain as I am that Hannah wouldn't want to be *that girl* dating the boss, I'm also just as certain that she wants to date me too.

I almost snort.

Dating is such a lame word for what I want from Hannah.

I want more than the occasional dinner out and texts in the evening.

I want everything.

Lifting my mug, I lean against the counter in the break

room and take a sip of my coffee while I pretend to read an email on my phone.

When I got home early yesterday morning, after spending a handful of hours sleeping in Hannah's tiny-ass bed with my body wrapped around hers, it hit me.

I don't want to wait.

I don't want to wait to tell her how much she means to me. How much she's always meant to me.

I don't want to wait years before I ask her to move in with me.

I don't want to wait at all.

We already lost so much time together. And if I think on it too much, I might just lose my mind. Or I might hire that guy Waller knows to go burn Essie's house down.

I take another sip of my coffee.

I'm not going to dwell on the past anymore.

It happened. It's over. And now —

The break room door opens, and my brown-eyed beauty walks in.

My lips curl up into a smile, but I stay exactly where I am.

Hannah is a whole new person now, just like I am. She's lived a life's worth of experiences, just like I have.

Our lives were so different.

Mine was on the road, playing ball professionally. The glamour, physical pain, money, fame. Never knowing who wants to be close to you for you or who is just inching closer to try and hitch a ride in your wagon.

Hers was here. So close to me, but completely out of reach. She lost people, gained a ward, then knit her family so closely around her she was never alone. The love in her home is palpable. And I want my house filled with that. I want to feel that warmth when I step through the front door.

"Morning." Her cheeks are already turning pink, and I hope she's thinking about my lips on hers.

"Good morning," I greet her in return.

An older guy, who I think works in billing, is sitting at one of the long tables in the room, and he lifts his eyes from his phone just long enough to say hello to Hannah.

In the week we've been in this new office space, I swear I've seen that man come in early every day just to sit in here and eat a pair of donuts. He's wearing a wedding ring, and I have to assume either his wife won't let him eat donuts at home or he doesn't like being at home.

Won't be me.

I push off the counter and take the few steps to the coffee maker.

Hannah darts a glance my way as she bends to put a container of food into the fridge.

"What'd you bring for lunch?" My tone is casual, but it still has her biting her lip.

She straightens and closes the door. "Just some leftover Chinese takeout."

I nod. "Sounds good."

She narrows her eyes the smallest amount as she comes closer to where I am. "Do you bring your own lunch? Or are you too fancy for that?"

"Fancy?" I grin. "I'm not too fancy. I'm just lazy. Which is why I spend half my paycheck on delivery fees."

She rolls her eyes at me. "Pretty sure you'd have to be ordering barrels of caviar for that to be true."

"Nah, the barrels make it taste funny."

She lets out a little laugh. "Just ham and cheese sandwiches, then."

I keep my eyes on hers, not missing the way she mentioned

it so lightly. "Best tasting thing there is. With maybe one exception."

Hannah's gaze drops to my lips.

That's right, Babe. When I say taste, you look at my mouth.

Clearing my throat, I reach up and open the mug cupboard for her.

We're a clean energy company, so everything we have is reusable, and some chucklehead thought it would be great to have nothing but bright yellow dishes and mugs. Some have our logo, some are secondhand, some are handmade, but they all have yellow on them.

Hannah wiggles her fingers as she selects her mug for the day, choosing a ceramic one covered in vibrant shades of yellow that was definitely made by hand.

I'm not surprised that's the one she chose.

Donut Man is paying us no attention, so I stay where I am and watch Hannah make her coffee.

She fills her mug, leaving about an inch of space, then holds the pot up toward me. "Need a top off?"

I dip my chin and hold my MinneSolar branded mug out to her.

She looks at it, seeing that it's already full, but still tips the pot and adds a splash.

Hannah glances back at my mug as she puts the pot on the burner. "Plain black?"

I lift my coffee and smirk at her over the rim. "Four sugars."

Her brows jump up at my admission.

"Is there something wrong with that, Miss Utley?"

"Of course not, Mr. Lovelace. It's just with the whole athlete thing..." Her eyes travel down my body. Before they move back up, I pull my shoulders back just enough to make my chest look bigger. "I figured you more for a *no sugar* type."

"Back in my playing days, that was mostly true. But that's

the nice thing about being retired. I can eat whatever I want now."

She hums and moves to the fridge to take out a short carton of half-and-half, then uses it to gesture around the room. "I'm not sure you understand what *retired* means."

"Yeah, well, golf was never my thing. Plus, my buddy and I have a bet going on whose company can get more awards each year."

"Awards?" Hannah removes the cap from her little carton and pours about a third of an inch worth into her mug.

"No specific award, just achievements in general. Top fifty lists, that sort of thing," I tell her, referring to my never-ending cycle of bets with Waller.

Hannah returns the carton to the fridge, then looks at the drawer I'm standing in front of.

I know what she wants, but instead of moving so she can get a clean spoon, I take the one from my mug.

Another glance shows that we're still alone with Donut Man, who is focused on his donuts, so I put the spoon in my mouth.

I close my lips around it and pull it free before I hold it out for Hannah to take.

She darts her eyes around the room, but seeing the same thing I do, she takes it and puts it into her mug.

And that's when the door to the break room opens.

Hannah shifts, like she's going to jump away from me, reminding me of after the car accident.

"Don't react." I say it so only she can hear me.

I don't know who walked in, but nothing we're doing right now is inappropriate. We might be standing a little closer than total strangers would, but I'm friendly with everyone.

I turn my head, finding Brandon walking across the room.

Okay, so maybe I'm not friendly with *everyone*.

"Morning." I nod to the man because I'm still civil.

He nods back, then looks at Hannah. "Morning. Did you have a good weekend?"

"Really good," she answers without hesitating.

I lift my coffee and take another drink, covering my smile.

"Uh, that's nice," Brandon replies like the dumbass he is. "Mine was good too."

Too bad no one asked you.

He goes to the fridge and takes a tall can out of the door.

I almost roll my eyes. What sort of grown-ass man has a *cotton candy flavored* energy drink to start his day?

"Heading out?" I hold up my arm for Hannah as though she was waiting for me to leave, and I'm insisting she goes first.

She nods. "Yeah, best get to work."

As we walk across the room, Donut Man finally stands. "Welp, if the boss is getting after it, then I should too."

I feel a slight alarm at him paying attention to what's going on around him. But something tells me that even if he knew the entirety of my history with Hannah, he still wouldn't tell anyone.

FIFTY-FIVE
HANNAH

I'm shoving open my office door, ready to toss my armful of things onto my desk, when I freeze.

Because sitting on said desk is a mug of coffee.

The same mug I used yesterday, filled nearly to the brim with the perfect shade of coffee.

Warmth fills my chest.

Maddox.

Seeing him yesterday morning in the break room wasn't enough.

I need more of him.

The damn man is such a pleasure to be around that I miss him anytime he's not in the same room as me. Which is almost always.

Wanting the moment to myself, I step the rest of the way into my office and use my foot to push the door shut.

After I set my things down, I pick up the coffee.

It's still steaming but not so hot I can't try it. And the first sip confirms what I already assumed. It's perfect.

I want to return the favor. Or at least tell Maddox thank you. But there's no way for me to do that.

Sure, I could walk to his office. But I have no legitimate reason to be there. And walking through the whole office carrying a coffee for Maddox would be like slapping a neon sign on my back saying *I'm flirting with the boss*. And I certainly couldn't say I'm bringing him a coffee because he made me a coffee.

I have no idea how Maddox got this to my office without anyone seeing, but I'm sure he did.

I could always email Maddox to say thanks. But I've taken those stupid mandatory training courses, so I know all company emails are saved somewhere, and I don't need anyone intercepting nonwork emails between me and the owner of the company.

Maddox might have an office phone number I could find. But what if someone other than him answers? And if someone else answers, they can probably see who's calling, so I couldn't just hang up.

I spent hours wrapped up in Maddox's arms while we lay in my bed, yet I don't have his number.

A tendril of unease unfurls in my mind, suddenly morphing into panic.

I don't have his number.

I put the coffee down and pick up the first folder I can find.

Maddox and I work together.

He knows where I live.

He has my phone number off my résumé.

We won't lose touch again.

But...

I spin around and stride back out of my office.

People are starting to settle in, and about half the cubicles are full, but no one pays attention to me.

I keep my expression relaxed as I walk past the conference room, where it all started, and to the back, where all the executive offices are.

I've never been all the way back here, and as that fact sinks in, I start to slow.

Almost all the office's back here have their doors open and their lights on.

I slow even more.

Which way would Maddox be?

Then I hear him. That deep voice I recognize from my dreams.

Turning toward the sound, I cross to the far corner.

As I get closer, I see his name written on the plaque attached to his door.

Corner office. Duh.

I can't tell if he's talking to a person or if he's on his phone, but there's really no other way to do this, so I step into his open doorway.

The office is large. A couch with a coffee table sits on the near side of the room, a desk and two visitor's chairs at the opposite end, and the two outer walls are nothing but glass.

Maddox is standing behind his desk, looking handsome as always.

The movement of my appearance catches Maddox's attention, and he drifts his gaze past the other man standing in front of his desk to meet mine.

This is a bad idea.

I shouldn't have —

"Ah, Hannah." Maddox holds his hand out toward me, like he's been waiting for me to arrive.

"Morning." I say it to both of them, recognizing the other man as the director of sales. "I have those files you wanted to go over." I lift the folder, as if email hasn't been invented yet and I had to hand deliver the documents.

"Come in," Maddox tells me, then turns to the other man. "If you get any pushback, let me know."

The man nods. "Will do." Then he smiles and steps around me, out the door.

I want to shut the door to make our conversation private, but Maddox was just in here talking to someone with the door open, so I leave it as it is.

He gives me a crooked smile. "Would you like to sit? I can't remember how much time you said this would take."

With my back to the open door, I roll my eyes at him.

He starts to chuckle but catches it by clearing his throat.

Stopping in front of his desk, I pick up the fancy pen sitting next to his laptop. "I just need to point out a few things. Shouldn't take long."

I open the folder I brought.

It's empty.

Maddox grins. "By all means."

I pull the cap off the pen, then write on the inside of the blank folder.

Please give me your phone number.

FIFTY-SIX
MADDOX

My smile drops.

I read her words a second time.

Please give me your phone number.

How the fuck did we let that happen again?

I swallow and lift my gaze to hers.

Her lips are pressed together, and I can see the stress in her features.

I'm sure she felt this same crash of anxiety when she realized she didn't have it.

I don't waste a moment pulling out my phone and sending her a text.

I saved her information off her résumé but never shared my number back with her. Like a fucking idiot.

There's no answering notification or vibration, and Hannah doesn't move, so I'm guessing she left her phone in her office.

"You're correct." I strive for my usual business voice. "An oversight on my part. Good catch."

"Thank you." Her posture softens, then she reaches for the pen again.

And thank you for the coffee.

I take the pen from her hand and pull the folder closer so I can write back.

I accept hugs as payment.

Hannah bites her lip as she takes the pen back.

Put it on my tab.

Remembering how our last hug went, I'll definitely take her up on it.

I close the folder and slide it back over to her. "If you need anything more on this, I'll be out of the office tomorrow."

Disappointment crosses her features.

I don't want to make her sad, but I do like her reaction to knowing I won't be here.

"Appreciate the heads-up." She picks up the empty folder and steps back from my desk.

"Have a nice morning, Hannah."

"You too, Mr. Lovelace."

Unable to help myself, my eyes stay locked on Hannah's ass until every glorious inch of her is out of sight.

FIFTY-SEVEN
HANNAH

Back in my office, I debate for only a moment before sticking the folder into my paper shredder.

It's over the top, but I don't want to leave anything for anyone to use against me.

Not that I really think anyone would actually care if they knew Maddox and I are... whatever we are.

As my computer wakes up, I take another sip of my coffee — not caring that it's cooled down significantly — and pull my phone out of my purse.

> Unknown: Save this number, Little Bunny.

There's another text he must've sent after I left his office.

> Unknown: I should have given you this the day of the interview. When you hid from me before getting on the elevators.

My mouth drops open.

> Me: You saw that?

> Unknown: You were acting like you didn't know me. Of course I followed you.

I bite my lip.

> Me: Following an unsuspecting girl... Really showing off those Big Bad Wolf behaviors.

I quickly select the option to save his contact. I start to type out Maddox, then decide better of it.

> BB Wolf: Come over this weekend.

I read the text again, and my heart rate kicks up.

> BB Wolf: Friday evening for dinner.

> BB Wolf: And Saturday morning for breakfast.

> BB Wolf: And if your family doesn't mind, just stay all the way through to breakfast on Sunday.

A nervous laugh bubbles out of me, and I glance out my open door to verify no one is straining their necks to look at me over the cubicle walls.

> Me: I'll come over Friday for dinner.

I absolutely intend to stay for breakfast on Saturday, but I'll let him wonder about it.

After setting my phone down, I log into my computer and open my email.

A new email sits at the top of my inbox. From Maddox.

I click on it, nervous that he might be sending me something inappropriate, but it's to the whole office. Letting us know he'll be providing lunch on Thursday. And that it's not mandatory or formal, just giving a heads-up to those who usually bring their own lunch that they won't need to that day.

FIFTY-EIGHT
MADDOX

Texting hasn't been enough.

I drum my fingers against my thigh as I stand in the break room.

I need to see her.

Yesterday, I was across town all day, meeting with my financial adviser, and then this morning, I got pulled into a call before I even left the house, so I left late and just got here a bit ago.

The food arrived at the same time I did, so instead of heading right to Hannah's office like I wanted to, I followed the caterers.

But now the food is set up. People are starting to file in, grabbing the food they want, and if I don't sit down soon, it's going to look weird.

I pull my phone out of my pocket.

Me: Get your ass to the break room.

I watch Brandon's eyes move over to my food wrappers, where I have the same bag of chips. Only mine is empty.

He takes a drink of his Coke, then eats another chip.

Hannah and the ladies next to me share a look, and I know we're all thinking the same thing.

This fool would rather choke down food that's too spicy for him than risk looking *weak*. A real case of death by machismo.

Moron.

FIFTY-NINE
HANNAH

Maddox still has his foot hooked behind mine.

I know I should move, because even though it's unlikely for anyone to see it, it's not impossible. One dropped napkin, and we'd be outed.

But I'm not quite ready to lose contact yet.

I knew I wanted to see him, but I hadn't realized how badly until I walked through that door. So I want to savor this short time together.

I shift my other foot closer until Maddox's ankle is pressed between mine.

Sitting here across the table from him, I can't help but think of that first lunch out together.

I'm not still upset about it. I'm just upset that I spent the time being mad and hurt when I could have just been soaking in his presence.

"Hannah." His deep rumble pulls my attention up.

I hadn't realized I'd been staring at his chest.

I blink, and the project managers snicker next to Maddox.

My cheeks start to heat. "Sorry, totally zoned out there for a second."

"It's alright. Lunch does that to me too sometimes." He smirks at me. "Just wondering if you're done. I can take your trash."

I look at the table and see Maddox has balled up his wrappers.

"Oh, that's alright. I should get back to work." I scoot my chair back and gather up my own garbage.

Brandon is still swapping bites of chips with sips of his drink, so thankfully he doesn't try to get up at the same time.

I know we need to keep this thing between us a secret — so long as we work together — but I'd love to make my feelings for Maddox known, if only to get Brandon to finally back off and leave me in peace.

"See ya," I tell the people around me, then stand from my chair.

Maddox uses his long strides to beat me to the waste cans, and I sort out the trash, compost, and recycling.

I follow him at a normal distance, and Maddox opens the door to the break room and holds it for me to pass through ahead of him.

"So, Hannah." Maddox moves so we're walking side by side. "Did you have a nice morning?"

"Nothing to complain about." I glance up at him. "How about you?"

His brows raise. "Oh, I have plenty to complain about."

"That so?"

He nods. "I had to wake up without my girl at my side."

I bite my lip and keep my eyes ahead of us. "Sounds hard."

Maddox snorts. "It was."

"Oh my god." I elbow him in the side. "You're such a frat boy."

"Now, now," he fake admonishes. "Football is not a frat."

"Sure it's not." I widen my eyes.

Maddox pulls something out of his pocket and holds it out to me.

I can't help the little laugh that comes out. "What is that?"

"A cookie." He looks down and grimaces.

I can sort of recognize it as the ones we just had at lunch. The soft cookies were wrapped in clear plastic and were delicious, but this one is squished into the shape of a stubby taco.

Using his other hand, he tries to flatten it. "It got a little mashed up."

"A little," I snort. "How long has that been in your pocket?"

"Just since the food got here." Having formed it back into the shape of a cookie, Maddox holds it out for me. "They're my favorite." He pats his pocket. "I have another for myself."

I poke at one of the raisins through the cling film. "First the sugary coffee, now raisin cookies? You're full of surprises, Maddox Lovelace."

When he doesn't reply, I look up.

He's staring down at me, the humor gone from his features.

"What's wrong?" I ask quietly, even though the cubicles closest to my office are empty.

His jaw works before he whispers. "I want to kiss you."

"We shouldn't," I whisper back, taking a step into my office. "But I want to, too."

SIXTY-FOUR
MADDOX

Using my grip on Hannah's hand, I tug her in front of me so her back is to my bed.

I loosen my fingers and step back. "Take your clothes off, Hannah."

Her chest is rising and falling in time with my own.

She hesitates for just a moment.

"You're fucking perfect. I already know that. Now show me."

Hannah huffs out a breath. "I expect you to get naked too."

I grin at her. "Oh, I'm gonna be fucking naked."

To prove my point, I reach behind myself and grip the collar of my T-shirt. Then, in one motion, I pull it off my body and toss it to the floor.

Hannah's eyes move to my chest. Down my arms. Across my stomach.

I can feel her gaze trailing over my tattoos. Probably remembering how I didn't have them that first time together.

"You can study them later," I tell her as I undo my belt

buckle. With a swift yank, I snap the belt free from my pants. "Catch up."

Her lips part on a gasp, but she complies.

Hannah grips the hem of her shirt and pulls it up over her head.

I groan.

Her tits are practically spilling out of her bra.

I'm definitely watching that movie with my head on her chest tonight.

We pull our zippers down at the same time. My jeans and her shorts. And together, we let them drop to the floor.

I step out of my pants, leaving me in nothing but boxers. The thin cotton does nothing to hide the fact that my cock is straining to be freed.

Hannah pauses again. In her pretty white panties and light pink bra.

"Naked, Hannah." I grip my length through my boxers. "I'm not touching you until you're completely naked."

Hooking my fingers in the waistband, I shove my boxers down.

My length bobs free, and I grip the base. Squeezing. Needing the touch, but also not wanting to blow before I get inside my girl.

Hannah reaches a hand for me.

"No." I stop her with my words even as I drag my grip up my cock. "Take them off."

She makes a sound that might be a complaint, but her hands go behind her back.

A moment later, her bra drops to the ground, and it's my turn to make a sound. Only there's no complaint in my tone.

Her fingers twitch, then she pushes her panties down her legs.

She has to bend over to get them off, and her tits sway with the movement. And I amend my previous statement, I'm starting with her tits in my mouth.

SIXTY-FIVE
HANNAH

My hands are trembling.

I've never felt so ready and so exposed at the same time.

But when I straighten, there's no time to overthink, because Maddox is there.

He's right there.

He grips my sides, and the tip of his hard cock presses against my lower belly.

I arch my neck, eyes closing, ready for his mouth on mine.

But the cock against my belly slips away, and before I can open my eyes, lips close around one of my nipples.

My body jerks at the contact, but Maddox holds me in place.

He rumbles out a sound of approval, and when my eyes finally focus, I see him on his knees in front of me.

He's so tall that, in this position, my breasts are at just the right height.

His tongue laps across my peak as he sucks more of my tit into his mouth.

I sway.

"Maddox." His name is a plea, and I reach for him, needing to steady myself.

He sucks again, then pulls his mouth free. "So perfect," he mumbles, then latches himself on to my other breast.

I dig my fingers into his shoulders.

I want to touch him. Want to kiss him. Want to feel more of him.

But I don't want him to stop.

He shifts his hands on my sides, sliding one around to my back, holding me against his working mouth.

He licks and sucks and makes sounds against my skin.

And he slides the other hand down my hip, then around until he's palming my ass.

Then lower. And lower, until he's reaching between my legs from behind.

The first brush of his fingers against my sex makes my knees weak, and I tighten my hold on him to stay upright.

He lightly traces my seam, and it's still enough to shoot electricity through my system.

"Holy shit," I pant. Then I change my hold on his shoulders, and I try to pull him up. Try to pull him off me because I need to touch him too.

Teeth graze over my nipple, and I throw my head back.

My body is tense, everything clenching, but that doesn't stop Maddox from shoving a finger inside me.

A cry leaves my mouth.

Maddox slides his finger deeper.

"Please," I pant. "God, Maddox, please."

He slides the hand on my back to my hip, and I think he might release me. But he shuffles forward. He presses himself against me, his mouth still sucking my breast, but his face pushing me backward.

I take one step, the finger inside me feeling so foreign with the movement, but then I'm bumping against the mattress.

And I'm falling.

Maddox slips his finger free just as I land on the bed, then he uses both hands to shove me back onto the mattress.

His shoulders are already between my thighs, and as he shifts closer, I spread my legs.

I'm no longer worried about what he might see. There is no room for self-consciousness when a man is acting this feral. This starved.

"That's my girl," Maddox murmurs. Then his mouth is on me again, only this time it's like he promised, with his face between my thighs.

He licks me. From my entrance to my clit.

He does it again. And again.

I can't stop squirming. Can't stop reaching for him. My fingers tugging at his hair.

"Jesus, Hannah." He licks again. "Such a slick little pussy." Something presses against my entrance, and it feels like two fingers this time. "Tell me I can come inside you bare again." He pushes his fingers into me. Just an inch. Then two. "Tell me, and I'll give you what you want." Another inch.

I nod.

I nod, and I nod, and I tug on his hair.

"Words, Babe." He jiggles his fingers, and I just...

I let go of his hair and reach down between us.

My fingers brush over my clit, once, then his other hand snatches my wrist, pulling my hand away.

"Tsk, tsk." He shakes his head and pulls his fingers free from my pussy.

I let out a whine. "No. Wait!"

Maddox climbs to his feet. "It was a simple question, Hannah."

I can't remember the question because all I can think about now is the oversized cock attached to the oversized man standing between my spread legs.

"Scoot up."

I blink at him. "What?"

His smile is devilish as he leans over me. "Scoot up on the bed, Hannah." He lightly closes his fingers around my throat. "I was going to have you come on my tongue first, but since you just can't seem to wait, you're going to come on my cock." His grip flexes, and I feel each fingerprint in my core.

I start to scramble backward, farther onto the mattress.

Maddox drops his hold on me, but he climbs with me, crawling onto the bed over me. His movements match my own.

"Now tell me I can come inside you."

Fucking hell.

I nod. "You can come inside me."

He's positioned his body between my legs, but I widen my thighs farther, urging him closer.

"That's my good girl."

He smiles down at me, and it's so soft. So sweet. I want to cry.

"Now lift your hips."

I plant my feet on the mattress and do as he says.

Maddox slides a pillow underneath me, then presses his palm against my belly, pinning me down.

"I'm going to get in as deep as I can, Little Bunny. I need to feel you everywhere." He shifts his hips forward, and the blunt tip of his dick presses against my entrance. "You can tell me if it's too much." He notches inside me, then lowers his mouth until it's a breath away from mine. "But I know you can take me. Because you were fucking made for me."

His lips press against mine as he thrusts his hips forward, and stars explode in my vision.

My body arches.

He's so big. Bigger than he felt last week. Bigger than I remember.

But the fullness only heightens the delicious sensation of stretching around him.

His tongue slides across my parted lips before curling into my mouth.

And I can taste it. I can taste my arousal in his kiss.

And I snap.

I close my lips around his tongue and suck it into my mouth. My hands pull at him. My nails dig into the bare skin of his sides. My feet hook around his lower back, and I pull him closer.

Maddox rocks his hips, and his cock hits even deeper.

His hips are flush against me, and his heavy balls are against my ass. He couldn't get any deeper if he tried, and I couldn't take any more if I wanted to.

He's at the end of me. I can feel it.

Because you were fucking made for me.

Pleasure swirls around us.

Maddox pulls out, then shoves back in.

We were made for each other.

He does it again. Quicker this time.

A perfect fit.

Tears build behind my closed lids.

Maddox is my perfect fit.

SIXTY-SIX
MADDOX

She's clinging to me. Taking every inch of me. Moaning and clawing and pulling me to her.

She's fucking amazing.

Hannah is amazing.

My match.

My other half.

My missing piece.

I open my mouth, angling my head to taste more of her.

My hips never stop moving. I couldn't make them stop if I wanted.

My cock slides in and out of Hannah's sweet pussy.

I need the friction.

Need the heat.

I need her.

Heat and desire and a feeling of home have my balls squeezing and emotion building inside my chest.

Her breasts are pressed against me. Her feet are bruising against my back. And I know she feels it too. This thing between us.

The pull.

I shift my weight onto one arm and reach the other down between our bodies.

"My Hannah," I say against her lips.

My fingers find her little bundle of nerves, and I swipe across it.

She arches, and her pussy tightens around me.

"My perfect girl." I slam my hips into her, making her bounce beneath me.

Her hips roll, and I pull my head back enough so I can look down at her.

Her eyes are squeezed shut, and tears trail down her cheeks.

Pride swells inside me.

I knew she felt it.

And now she knows it.

She belongs to me.

"Open your eyes," I command. "Open your eyes and let me see you come."

Hannah snaps her eyes open, and I roll her clit between my fingers, shoving myself as deep as I can go.

Staring up at me, she cries my name as she explodes.

SIXTY-SEVEN
HANNAH

An orgasm stronger than anything I've ever experienced slams into me.

Maddox is above me, watching me, and it's like a damn has broken between us.

He rolls my clit one more time, then he pulls his hand away and falls on top of me.

Maddox shoves his arms underneath me, hugging me to him as his muscles flex.

"Fuck, Babe. Fuck." He pumps into me.

I feel more tears trail from my eyes as he groans low and deep.

His body tenses, and I cling to him harder, pressing my face into his neck to savor the feeling of it.

The way his pulsing cock feels inside me.

The way he's holding me so tightly as he comes undone.

It feels like so much more than fucking.

It feels like... a connection.

Thick, comforting emotions blanket me, and I take a deep breath.

Maddox does the same.

When he exhales, he rocks his hips one last time.

I press my lips to his sweat-dampened neck, and he nuzzles the side of his face against my hair before turning his head and pressing a long kiss against my temple.

"I'm never letting you go, Hannah Bunny." He presses another soft kiss against me. "I hope you understand. I'm never letting you go."

SIXTY-EIGHT
MADDOX

Instead of tensing at my words, Hannah goes lax beneath me.

I don't think she fully understands, not truly, how much I mean it. But that's okay because I'll show her.

I press my lips to her temple again.

I can't fucking help myself.

It's on the tip of my tongue to tell her the truth. That I love her. But I don't want to say it too soon, and risk her thinking I'm insincere.

But in reality, I know it's not too soon because I've known this beautiful woman for fifteen years. We just lost each other for a moment.

I press my lips against her warm skin again, holding them there.

Hannah presses her own kiss to that spot where my neck meets my shoulder.

The movement causes her muscles to flex around me, and it makes my dick twitch. Which makes my whole body twitch.

Hannah snickers, and that starts the cycle again.

"Just hold still," I grunt. The tensing muscles are too much on my oversensitive cock.

"Sorry," she laughs, and her vibrating body makes me groan.

I dislodge my arms from underneath her and plant my hands next to her head to push myself up.

Looking down, I take her in. Her big tits. Her flushed chest. The smudged makeup around her eyes.

She wasn't crying from sadness or pain. It was from overwhelming emotion. I know it was because I felt it too.

I shift back and brush my thumb across one of the tear trails. "Perfect."

Hannah bites her lip, and I drag my thumb down her cheek until I'm pulling her lip free from her teeth.

Then, because her mouth is right there, I lower mine to meet it.

Our sighs mingle as our lips touch, but when I pull back, Hannah shifts and scrunches up her nose. Like a goddamn bunny.

"Maddox?"

"Hmm?" I tap my fingertip to her nose.

"We're making a mess."

"Huh?" I look lower to where we're connected. "Oh."

I pull partway out, looking at the mess she's referring to.

"Maddox." She smacks my arm with a snort. "Get off."

I give her a sad look. "In my twenties, I could've. But now..." I shake my head.

Hannah rolls her eyes. "Oh my god, just get your giant cock out of me."

My bark of laughter is unexpected, which causes me to slip the rest of the way out.

Hannah snaps her legs together as soon as I'm out of the

way, but with her knees up, I'm still treated to a wonderfully messy view.

I know better than to take naked photos of anyone anywhere, but damn, I'm fucking tempted.

Instead, I drag my eyes up to meet Hannah's. "Stay put."

"I'm —"

I stride across the room toward the bathroom. "One second."

Maybe eight seconds later, I'm back with a damp washcloth.

"I can do it." Hannah tries to sit up as I near, but her butt is still up on the pillow, making it difficult.

"Let me do it." I tap her knee. "Open."

"Open," she grumbles in a voice that's meant to be a mockery of mine. But it's just cute.

"Hannah."

"Fine!" She slaps her hands over her eyes and drops her knees apart.

SIXTY-NINE
HANNAH

This man is so infuriating.

But even as I keep my hands over my eyes, I have to admit he's gentle. Even if it's all overly familiar.

"There." Maddox rubs a hand up the inside of my thigh. "Gimme your hand."

Lowering my palms, I peek up and see him, still completely naked, holding a hand out to me.

I take it, and he pulls me up to a sitting position. Then I climb off the bed.

Maddox glances at our discarded clothes but leaves them and moves to pick my bag up off the floor. "You're welcome to wear whatever you want. But after that" — he nods to the bed — "I'm putting sweats on." He holds the bag out to me. "If you didn't bring anything comfy, I can lend you something."

I take the bag and hold it in front of my body, feeling a little bit shy and a little bit cold, being completely nude in an air-conditioned room. "I have pajamas."

He gestures to his bathroom. "You can get dressed in here if you'd like. I just need to grab my clothes."

I follow Maddox's bare ass into his bathroom. And what a bathroom it is. White marble counters. A white claw-foot tub. Giant glass shower. Double vanities with floor-to-ceiling cabinets on either side of the sinks.

Maddox turns away from me and heads toward a massive closet.

With his back to me, I hurry across to the other door that I'm sure is concealing the toilet. I'm glad Maddox is so comfortable with nudity, but it's very bright in here.

CLEANED up in a pair of soft gray pants, a comfy bralette, and an old Minnesota Biters T-shirt, I exit the bathroom.

Maddox is sitting on the edge of his bed — which has been put back to rights — looking at his phone. And I have to smile when I see he's quite literally wearing the same outfit as me. Only his pants are darker, and his shirt has the newer branding.

He looks up, and his jaw works as he takes me in.

"Well." He stands and starts to cross the room. "I like that."

I take a step back. "This old thing?" I shrug.

"Where are you going?" Maddox keeps stalking me.

I take another step back and hold my palms out. "Stay back, you animal."

He closes the distance, not stopping until my hands are pressed against his stomach. "Give me one good reason."

"One, you're not in your twenties anymore. Remember?" When he makes a sound and pushes closer, I add, "And two, I'm hungry and was promised dinner."

Maddox makes a show of heaving out a sigh. "Fine." He

grabs my wrist, then entwines our fingers as he leads me out of the room. "Want a quick tour first, or want to wait?"

"Tour," I answer automatically. I am hungry. But I'm also curious.

We walk back down the hall that brought us here and past the staircase to the other side of the house.

Maddox slows at the first door, which is already open.

"This is one of the guest suites." We step inside the room. "Doesn't get used much."

I can feel Maddox shrug next to me.

"It's really nice," I say truthfully.

It's the same white walls and dark floors as everything else, with big windows and classic furniture.

Maddox leads me across the room and flips the light on in the attached bathroom. Which is just as nice. White subway tile with black grout covers the walls, making the room classic and pretty.

We move back out into the hallway, and Maddox shows me another guest suite that looks nearly identical. Then there's an unused spare office and yet another guest suite.

It's all very nice.

And very empty.

It feels like I'm in a fancy hotel that hasn't opened yet.

Finished with the second floor, Maddox leads us back to the stairs.

"I got the extra space so my family would have a place to stay when they visited. But my parents have yet to downsize, and anytime my brother even acts like he's gonna stay here instead of at my parents' house, my mom acts like her life is ending."

His description makes me huff out a laugh. "Moms can be dramatic."

Maddox squeezes my fingers, reminding me we've been holding hands this entire time. "Ruth seems reasonable."

I scoff. "I'm sorry, what part of anything she did or said was reasonable?"

"Telling Chelsea she could have boys over when she turned thirty-five."

SEVENTY
MADDOX

Walking Hannah through my house highlights just how little of it I actually use. But of course, she's too nice to point out the wasted space.

"I'll show you the basement later," I tell her as I lead her toward the kitchen.

She looks over the items I have out on the island.

"Have a seat," I gesture to the stools at the island and finally release her hand.

Hannah climbs onto one of the seats and swivels it so she's facing me across the counter. "What are we having?"

"One of the few things I know how to make." I turn the burner on under the pot I already filled with salted water, then move to the fridge and pull out the rest of the ingredients. "Lemon butter noodles with shrimp."

"Mm, that sounds amazing."

I glance over to see her smiling.

"I made it a lot while I was playing, usually with chicken, but I saw you eating shrimp at your mom's birthday dinner, so I figured you'd be okay with it."

"I'm definitely okay with shrimp. Is there anything I can do?"

Shaking my head, I slice one of the lemons in half and quarter the other. "Just sit there and look pretty."

Hannah sighs. "Always a charmer."

"Just speaking the truth is all."

"Uh-huh."

I pause as I'm reaching for the parsley. "Sorry, it's been a while since I've hosted anyone." I set the knife down. "Would you like something to drink? I've got water, there's wine in the cellar —"

"Water is perfect." Hannah cuts me off before I can list every liquid in the house.

"Ice?"

"No thanks."

I narrow my eyes at her as I take two glasses out of the cupboard. "Weirdo."

Hannah snorts but watches me fill her glass. "How long have you lived here?"

While I cook dinner, I answer her questions. Telling her how I bought the lot not long after moving back to play for the Biters. I explain what a nightmare it was to go furniture shopping with my mother. How my dad showed up literally every day during construction, just to watch from the yard because he's a bored retiree.

Hannah grins at my stories and accepts a glass of whiskey on ice when I pour one for myself. It is Friday night, after all, and I have my girl in my house, no better reason for a celebratory drink.

"What are you doing?" Hannah asks when I pull a large tray out of the pantry.

"We're not eating here" is all I tell her as I plate up two dishes containing heaping piles of lemony noodles and sautéed shrimp.

"Okay. Where are we eating?" I see her glance toward the back of the house, but we aren't going outside either.

I set my beverages on the tray, then tip my head toward her glasses. "Grab your drinks, Babe."

She slides off the stool and does as she's told.

Hannah follows me as I walk past the main living room and down the hallway that leads to a set of rooms underneath my bedroom.

The first room is my home office.

The next room...

I pause. "Mind opening the door for me?"

Hannah looks at me suspiciously since the door isn't latched shut, but she moves ahead of me and uses her elbow to swing the door open.

And then she stops.

She just stops.

"What... What is this?" Her question is quiet.

"My study," I reply just as quietly. "Or you could call it my little library."

SEVENTY-ONE
HANNAH

It's not mine.

This room isn't mine.

It's his.

But...

I take one step forward as my heart shimmies up my throat.

"Maddox." I take another step. "It's..."

"You like it?" His tone holds a hint of hesitation, and I need him to stop that. Right now.

"Maddox." I turn to face him. "This is fucking magical."

His face cracks into a wide smile. "So... you like it?"

"Don't be ridiculous." I turn back to take in the room. "This is my new favorite place on earth."

I'm not even joking.

I step farther into the room.

The walls, where you can see them, are painted a deep green. But there's not much of it to see.

The wall opposite the door is all windows. The sun has set, so the dark panes reflect the room back at me.

And goddamn, this room is what dreams are made of.

There's a large, deep cushioned couch covered in blankets and pillows. In front of it is a rustic coffee table covered in candles. They aren't lit, but there's a box of matches sitting next to one of them.

The wall behind the couch is books. Nothing but books. The shelves reach all the way to the ceiling, and every shelf is stuffed full of books.

I turn my head.

The wall opposite is the same, with a rectangle carved out in the center of the shelves, where a TV is mounted. But every free inch is filled with more books.

"Where did you get them all?" I don't bother keeping the awe out of my voice.

Maddox shrugs. "Here and there."

The movement reminds me that he's holding a tray of food, so I shuffle over and take a seat on the couch, nearly sighing because it's just as comfortable as it looks.

As Maddox sets the tray down on the coffee table, I put my drinks down beside it and then tip my head back.

Hanging from the ceiling are bulbs. They're like those Edison bulbs, only they're perfectly round.

"Maddox." I shake my head, still looking up. "How..."

I want to ask how he made this room so alive when the rest of his house is so... not. But I can't ask that.

And it's not like the rest of the house is bad. It's stunning. It's huge. It's nicely furnished and finished. It just doesn't have any personality. Not like this room.

Maddox shuts the door, sealing us into the wonderful space.

"I don't come in here as much as I should." He answers my unasked question. "But I saw a photo once in a magazine I picked up while passing through an airport." He looks around the room as he sits next to me. "It's not exactly the same as this, but it's close."

"It's beautiful." I cross my legs on the large cushion and place my hand on his knee. "Thank you for showing me."

Maddox turns toward me. "I don't want to rush you. Or push you into anything too quick."

"You're not," I tell him before he can talk himself into thinking I don't want these moments together.

He places his hand over mine on his knee. "I don't have many regrets in my life, but the lost time between us, that's the biggest one I have."

Tender emotions twist between my ribs. "It's not your fault. We both..." I trail off.

We both made mistakes. And we both can see it. But I don't want to go there, not now. Not when we're here now.

"Maybe." He squeezes my fingers. "But we were supposed to do this."

"Do what?"

Instead of answering, Maddox reaches for our pasta and hands one of the plates to me. Then he grabs a remote.

As I lean back into the couch, the opening credits of a movie start to play.

And when I recognize them. When I understand what movie it is... I can't stop the single tear from trailing down my cheek.

Maddox settles next to me. "I'd still like you to finish reading it to me."

I press my lips together and nod. "I'd like that too."

Together, eating a delicious dinner and sipping Maddox's own brand of whiskey, fifteen years later than we'd planned, we watch *The Count of Monte Cristo*.

The body beside me shifts.

"Bed, Babe."

"Hmm?" I snuggle into Maddox.

His body vibrates with a chuckle. "Bunny, I'm too old to sleep on the couch."

I poke a finger into his side. "You're only a year older than me."

"Uh-huh." Maddox leans forward, and my head slides down between his back and the back cushion of the couch. "Except my body is fucked from football."

I push against said body to sit upright and blink against the glow of the lights above us.

We both stayed awake for the movie, all the way to the end, both ignoring the multiple times the story made me cry.

Neither of us asked, and neither of us offered up the information, but I've already watched the movie countless times on my own. And I'm pretty sure Maddox has seen it before tonight too.

But when the final scene was over, we were both too comfortable to get up.

So we didn't.

And apparently we fell asleep.

Maddox bumps his shoulder against mine. "You get up first."

I put my feet on the rug with a yawn. "Why?"

"So you can help me up."

I snicker but comply.

Standing, I hold my hands out for Maddox, and he takes them.

I almost didn't expect him to pull with his full weight, but he does, and I nearly tip over on top of him.

I brace my legs, and Maddox stands with a groan. "Thanks, Bunny."

I help him gather all the empty dishes onto the tray. He insists on carrying it, even as he limps a little.

"You sure you're okay?"

"Uh-huh." He sets the tray on the kitchen counter. When I reach for the plates, he grabs me by the shoulders and turns me around. "Tomorrow. Now is bed."

Maddox turns off the lights as we go, and by the time we reach his bedroom, I'm ready to drop back into sleep.

I quickly use the bathroom and remove my bralette, then find Maddox sprawled on the bed, his bare chest exposed.

Climbing onto the mattress, I lift the covers to peek and find him in boxers.

"Naughty girl," Maddox says even though his eyes stay shut.

"Just curious." I shimmy under the blanket as he reaches over and turns off the last lamp.

"Come here. Get in your spot."

Your spot.

He says it like this is normal for us. Like I've curled up into his side more than once before. That it wasn't so long ago, sleeping on a trio of benches in the university library.

But I know exactly what spot he's talking about.

So, I move closer, facing Maddox, who's flat on his back. And when my front meets his side, I nestle my face in that spot where shoulder and chest meet.

Maddox curls his arm around my shoulders while I stretch my arm across his chest and hike my knee up so it's resting on his thigh.

"Good night, Hannah."

I press a kiss to his warm chest. "Night, Maddox."

Something soft wiggles against my aching cock, and I press into it.

"Jesus." Hannah's moan filters in through my half-asleep brain.

Hannah.

Here.

Pressed against my morning wood.

"Maddox?" Her voice sounds again.

"Hmm?" Eyes still closed, I reach for her, my hand landing on her hip.

I tug her against me.

During the night, we changed positions. And now I'm spooning her.

Hannah arches her back. "If you don't put that thing to use..."

Eyes opening, I roll forward, forcing Hannah to roll too until she's lying on her stomach beneath me.

"You want me to fuck you, Babe?" I keep her pinned as I

lift partially off her so I can yank her sleep pants and underwear down, exposing her ass.

"Yes." Her words are muffled by the mattress.

I reach down farther, sliding my hand between her thighs.

"Fuck," I groan. "You're already wet for me?"

She nods.

I rub my fingers against her opening, spreading the slickness.

"Were you rubbing this ass on my dick while I slept, getting yourself ready?"

Hannah nods again.

I feel like I should tease her a bit. Like I should drag this out.

But I'm so fucking hard it hurts.

I pull the front of my boxers down. "Reach down and play with that clit."

Gripping the base, I position my dick where I want it.

Hannah's ass lifts beneath me, and she lets out a groan, telling me her fingers are where she needs them.

I lower my hips, one glorious inch at a time.

Hannah's pussy swallows me up. Squeezing and clenching.

Once I'm buried all the way, I drop my chest onto her back.

My knees are on the mattress on either side of her hips, but I'm still putting a lot of my weight on her. "You okay, Bunny?"

She nods again, making some noises of agreement.

I lift my hips, then push my dick back in.

"Keep rubbing that clit for me," I tell her as I try to keep my motions steady. "My greedy girl, waking me up with this hot little pussy."

She moans.

Pushing all the way in, I roll my hips this time.

Hannah arches.

"I knew you were perfect." Her pussy is wrapped around

my dick like a vise. "Waking up horny for my cock. Getting wetter by the fucking second."

She clenches, hard, and I know she's doing it on purpose.

I smile against her hair.

"You trying to make me come, Bunny?" My breath is getting choppier, and the tightness builds in my balls. "Show me how good you are." I slam my hips against her ass. "Come for me now, Little Utley."

She tips over the edge. And I feel every contraction as her pussy pulses around my dick.

"Maddox."

Hearing her cry my name as she writhes below me is the last straw.

I thrust in one last time and unload deep inside her.

SEVENTY-FOUR
HANNAH

Maddox offered me the use of his shower, and even though I need to head home soon, I couldn't resist.

I know I'll never get a rain head shower in my bathroom at home, but after experiencing Maddox's freaking spa-level bathroom, I'm tempted to tape a hose to my ceiling. That felt like I was a damn fairy showering in the forest.

But alas, I'll just have to settle for showering every time I come over. What a hardship.

Considering I barely wore the outfit I came over in, I've changed back into my shorts and tank top and twisted my damp hair up into a bun.

It's not my best look, but Maddox has made me feel nothing but confident around him, so I don't stress about makeup.

I follow the scent of coffee down to the kitchen and find Maddox at the stove in a different pair of sweats and another T-shirt that clings to his muscles.

He looks up at my entrance. "Have a nice shower?"

I let my shoulders slump and my chin tip up. "Ohmygod, it was amazing."

Maddox smirks. "Glad to hear."

I circle around to stand beside him. "Pancakes?"

He bumps my hip with his own. "Don't get too excited. It's just a mix."

I bump his hip back. "Nothing wrong with that."

Maddox continues to flip and stack pancakes as I pour myself coffee, noticing the half-and-half already on the counter.

It's already been opened, but when I peek inside, it looks completely full. Like maybe he bought it just for me.

Unlike last night, Maddox lets me help with the food. So I warm the maple syrup in the microwave and, at his request, get the peanut butter out of the pantry.

Also unlike last night, we don't go to the amazing library room to eat but rather sit with our plates at the counter.

Maddox makes a stack six high, with layers of peanut butter between each pancake, then he smothers the whole thing with syrup.

He sees me eyeing it and gives me a bite. And that's enough to convince me to add a spoonful of peanut butter to my much shorter pile.

"Speaking of *The Count of Monte Cristo*," Maddox says, even though we weren't.

I arch a brow. "Yes?"

"I saw that book in your room." He tips his head and looks at me. "Do you have any idea how many late fees I have?"

I laugh as I admit, "I've felt so bad about taking library property. I was *this close* to mailing it back so many times."

"We can return it after we finish reading it."

I can't help but wonder about his assignment. "Did you get another copy? Or did you pick something else to read?"

"I checked out something else." Maddox shrugs. *I hate his answer.* "But it ended up sucking, so after I paid the fee for a lost book, I checked out another copy of The Count."

Too much relief comes with his words. "I read my copy too. A couple times." I glance over at him. "Sorry about the fee. I'd offer to pay you back, but I have a feeling you wouldn't let me."

"You don't have to pay me, but the first chance we have, I'm marching you into that library, and we're changing the records so it shows you're the one who *lost it*, not me."

"Uh-huh, sure."

Maddox takes a bite of pancake. "Do you still have my hoodie too?"

My fork pauses halfway to my mouth.

I forgot about the hoodie.

"What?" he asks, probably seeing the guilt on my features. "You better not have given it to another guy."

I choke on a laugh. "I did not give it to another guy."

"Then what happened to it?" Maddox leans his elbow on the counter.

"I burned it." I pop the piece of pancake into my mouth.

Maddox blinks at me. "You... burned it."

I nod.

"Any particular reason why?" He lifts his brows with the question.

"If you must know..."

Maddox sits up straight, turning back toward his food. "Maybe I don't want to know."

I continue anyway. "You went to some fancy charity event. And pictures from the night were plastered all over, and they showed you with this woman. And she was" — I wave my hand around — "freaking perfect. And it made me hate you a little. So I burned your sweatshirt in a bonfire."

Instead of looking sheepish, Maddox has a smirk on his face while he scoops up another bite of food.

"What?" I narrow my eyes.

"I know exactly what event you're talking about. And, that

My mouth pulls into a smile. "You're cute."

The tension in his shoulders vanishes, and a smirk forms on his lips. "Come sit on my lap and say that."

"Maddox," I hiss, glancing at the open door behind him.

He reaches back like he's going to swing the door shut.

"Stop it." I snag a paperclip off my desk and throw it at him. "You're gonna get me in trouble."

He catches the paperclip.

Of course he does.

"Throwing things, Miss Utley? Might need to send you to HR for some of those workplace training videos."

"Says the man who just asked me to sit on his lap," I deadpan.

Maddox twirls the paperclip in his fingers. "Maybe we should watch the movie together."

I press my lips together.

Maddox wasn't in the office yesterday, having meetings elsewhere, so now is the first time I've gotten to see him since I left his house Saturday morning.

"Sarah agreed to help with the books for some team her daughter skates on. And she offered to take me to lunch in exchange for helping her make sense of the spreadsheets." I try to get us back on topic. "And she'll be here any minute."

"Skating?"

"Ice skating."

"In the summer?"

I roll my eyes. "Oh my god, are you just here to pester me, or did you need something?"

He keeps his eyes on mine as he lowers his voice. "Can you come over Friday?"

It shouldn't make me so giddy to hear him ask. And he definitely shouldn't be asking me in the office. But I kinda love it.

I'm about to say yes when I remember I have plans. "I can't."

"Oh." Maddox looks so dejected I'm tempted to take him up on his first offer and climb into his lap.

"I want to." I tell him the truth. "But my mom has book club on Friday night, so Chelsea and I have plans to get pedicures and have a girls' night."

"Saturday, then?" Maddox narrows his eyes as I start to smile. "Why do I feel like I'm stepping into a trap?"

"Not a trap. Just a baseball game."

"Baseball," he groans. "First the hockey restaurant, now this."

"You're so dramatic," I laugh. "A bunch of people from Chelsea's school are going to the Kids game, and Mom has decided she doesn't want to go, so we have an extra ticket."

"But baseball is so boring," he complains. "Can't I just take you and Chelsea somewhere else? Literally anywhere else."

"Dramatic," I repeat. "And don't act like you don't like baseball. Everyone likes baseball."

Maddox sighs. "Fine, what time should I pick you up?"

"I think it starts at two —"

"What starts at two?" a female asks from the door. "Do you need to —" Sarah cuts off when she sees Maddox in my visitor's chair. "Oh. Uh." She looks up at me with wide eyes. "Sorry, did you want to postpone?"

"No, no, we're good," I tell her. "Maddox is talking about something else."

For a moment, I wonder if calling him that sounds too personal, but he's always telling everyone to call him by name, so it's really not that weird.

Maddox slips the paperclip into his pocket as he stands from the chair. "Hi, Sarah. Nice to see you again."

"Thanks," she breathes as she holds her hand out.

Then she must realize this isn't really a handshake moment, and she starts to lower her hand. But Maddox is already reaching out to take hers because he's accommodating like that, so she lifts her hand back up.

It's the most awkward interaction I've seen in a long time, and I have to avert my gaze to keep from cracking up.

"I just need to finish this email real quick." I focus on my screen.

"I'll get out of your hair, then," Maddox says. "You ladies have a nice lunch."

I lift my gaze to see Maddox pause at the doorway.

"Hannah, let's plan for noon."

"Alright," I agree with my most casual voice.

Sarah's back is to him, and she's staring at me with wide eyes, so she doesn't see when he winks at me.

Once he's gone, Sarah collapses into the chair Maddox just vacated. "I can't work for a man that attractive. It's just not right."

I glance at the empty doorway. "You're not wrong."

SEVENTY-SEVEN

HANNAH

"So…" I slow to a stop as the light ahead of me turns red. "Would you mind if Maddox came with us to the game tomorrow?"

Chelsea is typing out a text to one of her friends. "Don't care."

I watch her for a moment, trying to see if she's hiding a reaction from me. "Are you sure?"

Chelsea nods. "Yeah."

The light turns green, and I lift my foot off the brake.

Maybe she didn't hear me. "Maddox, the guy who came over during Grandma's birthday."

"Uh, duh. I know who Maddox is. He's kinda hard to miss."

Fair.

"And you're okay if he comes to the baseball game?" I glance over and find Chelsea looking at me.

"Still a yes." Her sass shouldn't warm my heart, but it does.

"Okay, if you're sure."

Chelsea sets her phone in her lap. "Are you two dating?"

"Well… technically… I don't know."

The tween next to me snickers. "Are you really trying to pull an *it's complicated* on me?"

I blow out a breath as I stop at another red light. "I'm not trying to *pull* anything. But" — I hold up a hand — "in my defense, it's true."

"Why is it complicated? Because you used to date?"

Internally, I kick myself. I should have just accepted her first yes and left it at that.

"We..." I trail off.

I can't tell my twelve-year-old that my past with Maddox was more of a one-night stand than an actual relationship.

"You know." She starts up again. "The more you evade answering my questions, the more I'm going to ask."

I send Chelsea a look before I start driving again. "I think you watch too many crime dramas."

She shrugs. "Maybe."

Sighing, I take the next turn onto the street with our preferred nail salon. "Maddox and I met in college."

"I thought you did online school?"

I nod. "I did for the last two years to get my accounting degree. But I went to HOP University for one week at the beginning of my junior year, and that's when I met Maddox."

"Just one week?" Chelsea turns in her seat, and I know I have her full attention now.

"Yeah. I was one week in when Grandma had her stroke."

"Oh." Her shoulders slump. "So you had to move back home, and you couldn't keep dating."

"Basically." It's a massive oversimplification of the story, but yeah.

"Well, that sucks."

I smile at her romantic little heart. "It did."

"And... that's why it's complicated?"

I tip my head back and forth. "I think we've worked

through all the old hurt feelings. But he's the owner of the company that I work for now, so he's basically my boss. And dating him would be against the rules."

"Ooh, so it's like a secret relationship." Chelsea sounds way too excited. "Like one of those Hallmark movies Grandma watches."

Images of Maddox bending me over the desk flash into my mind.

I clear my throat. "Kinda."

"If it's a secret, won't everyone see him at the game?"

She has a point. And I suddenly feel a bit like crying.

Spotting an open parking spot, I pull into it. "Maybe it's a bad idea."

"Fuck it."

I jerk my head over. "Chelsea!"

"What?" She lifts her hands. "Look, Aunt Hannah, I don't want you staying single forever because of me. And don't pretend I'm not the reason you don't date."

"That's not —"

She points a finger at me, and I stop talking.

"I've looked him up." My eyes widen. "Mad Dog Maddox." She rolls her eyes while she says his famous nickname. "He's basically a beast. Super strong. Big guy. Right?"

I nod. "Right."

"Seems kinda indestructible." She undoes her seat belt. "So, if anyone can break the curse, it's gotta be him."

Chelsea opens the car door and slides out, like she didn't just shift my entire world.

It's gotta be him.

SEVENTY-EIGHT
MADDOX

"Are you sure?" Hannah asks again.

"Yes," Chelsea and I answer at the same time.

Hannah tosses up her hands. "I'm just asking."

"For like the hundredth time," Chelsea huffs.

She's hardly even exaggerating.

Hannah called me last night, worried that going out in public was a bad idea.

I assured her it was fine.

She called me this morning, saying maybe I shouldn't come.

I told her I would be there at noon.

She spent the whole ride here twisting her hands together, suggesting I just drop them off at the stadium and that she'll figure out a ride home.

I ignored her.

Hannah looks up at me, worry written all over her face.

"Babe." I palm the back of her neck, keeping her at my side as we move with the crowd of people toward the entrance to the stadium. "Listen to me, yeah?"

She blinks and nods.

Chelsea peeks around Hannah to look up at me too.

"How many people are on the payroll at MinneSolar?"

Hannah huffs out a breath. "I think it's eighty-seven."

"It is." I don't know for sure, but I'm confident she's right. I tip my head toward the massive structure in front of us. "The Kids stadium holds thirty-nine thousand people. Even if every single one of our colleagues decides to come to today's game, what are the odds we'll run into them?" Before she tries to come up with the mathematical answer, I give her the reasonable one. "Low. The odds are low, Bunny."

"Bunny?" Chelsea makes a gagging sound.

I chuckle but keep addressing Hannah. "And what are the odds that all eighty-seven would be here today?"

She sighs. "Practically zero."

"So if we bring it back to the original equation and assume maybe one other MinneSolar employee is here, what are the odds we'll run into them?"

The look Hannah gives me is full of annoyance. "I understand what you're trying to do, but you also stand out in a crowd — from size alone — but you're also *famous*, which draws even more attention." She says the word famous like it's the most ridiculous thing in the world. "So if you want me to figure the odds of the situation, those factors need to be taken into consideration."

I lean forward to talk to Chelsea. "She always like this?"

Chelsea nods. "Always."

Hannah swats at me.

"If it makes you feel better." I pull a baseball hat from my back pocket and put it on my head. "I'll wear a disguise."

The hat is white, with the Kids's logo centered on the front, and I've had it forever, because Hannah was right, everyone likes baseball.

Chelsea and I thank him at the same exact time, making Maddox smile broadly. And he looks so... happy.

And fuck me, I think I'm addicted to seeing that smile.

Unaware of my thoughts, Maddox opens his bottle and tips it back.

His throat works as he swallows half the contents in one go.

It doesn't matter that he's retired. Doesn't matter that he's not training for hours a day anymore. He's still big and thick in all the ways that count. And in jeans, a T-shirt with a faded logo I don't recognize, and that fucking hat — the white contrasting with his dark hair — he's obnoxiously good looking. And like I said before, he looks exactly like the athlete he is.

I drop my gaze over to Chelsea. She's rolling her eyes at me, having caught me staring.

I mouth *shut up* at her, and she just rolls her eyes again.

"Okay, row eight." Maddox pokes Chelsea in the shoulder. "You first."

"Why me first?" Chelsea narrows her eyes at the big man.

"Because you're easy to see over," Maddox says seriously. "And if we trip, you can break our fall."

Chelsea grumbles something about "worst idea ever" as she turns to start down the stairs, but I don't miss the way her cheeks twitch.

Maddox presses his hand to my back. "You next."

"So you can crush me too?"

Maddox drags his fingertips up the back of my neck, sending a shiver down my spine.

I hurry forward, his deep chuckle following me.

Careful on the steps, I admit that it feels good to be out in public with Maddox. Like this is our normal, and we do it all the time.

I make a mental note to check on my job applications tomorrow. I've heard back from a few of the companies that I've since decided won't be a good fit, but there's still a handful that I think would work.

"What seats?" Chelsea stops at the end of our row.

"Um..." I start to pull out my phone to check.

"The three on the end," Maddox answers for me.

Chelsea moves to the third in, waving to a kid a few seats down.

It looks like the whole front chunk of this section is filled with Chelsea's classmates and their parents.

"Hey, Hannah!" A mom two rows down is turned around, looking up at us.

"Hey!" I know I know her, but I feel like a jerk because her name is slipping my mind. "How's your summer going?"

She shakes her head. "Chaotic. Too short. Too hot. Take your pick."

"Sounds about right," I laugh and shuffle into the row after Chelsea. "At least today isn't scorching."

The woman nods, but her attention is no longer on me. It's on the man behind me.

I let her stare as I stop in front of my seat.

I wore a wide-strapped red tank top today and a pair of stretchy but fitted jean capris. The fitted part was important because my hips are wide enough, and I'm trying to keep them contained, not add more fabric to increase my width.

This morning, as I was dressing, I had a vivid memory of the last time we came to a game here. We sat way up in the nosebleed seats, and I remember struggling to get my ass between the unforgiving armrests.

I'm not huge. Not the biggest girl there ever was. And most of the time, I feel totally fine in my body. But then I get into a situation — or seat — like that, and I remember the world isn't built for me.

Holding my breath, I lower myself.

My hips press against the armrests, and I have a moment of sheer panic that I'm not going to be able to sit here. But I let more of my weight press down, and my squishy bits adjust, letting me slide the rest of the way into the seat.

I fill my lungs.

It's not comfortable, but it's fine. And I'm not stuck perching on the edge of the seat like I did before.

Then Maddox sits down.

His hips are trim. But his frame is huge. So his butt fits into the seat just fine, but his knees touch the seat in front of him and his shoulder presses into mine, forcing me to lean over into Chelsea's seat.

He grunts, and shifts, and says something about "made for fucking children."

And suddenly, I don't feel too big anymore.

Biting my lip, I twist and look up at him. "You okay?"

He shifts. "I feel like Baymax stuck in that window."

I let out a startled laugh and shake my head. "How do you even know that reference?"

Maddox lifts his arm up around my shoulders. "What, a man can't enjoy a good animated film?"

"You're totally right. Sorry for judging."

"Uh-huh." Maddox looks down at me. "Babe. I take up too much space."

My humor fades. "No, you don't." I grip his thigh, squeezing. "You're perfect."

His giant grin catches me off guard. "Oh, Bunny." With the arm around my shoulders, he pulls me into his body and kisses the top of my head. "I appreciate you saying that. But I need something else from you."

He loosens his grip, and my eyes drop to his lap before snapping back up to meet his gaze.

And he looks like he's trying *really hard* not to laugh. "I'd appreciate you for that too. But try to control yourself. This is a family sport."

I flick his leg. "You're the one —"

He gives my ponytail a little tug. "I need you to switch seats with your mini me."

Spacing on what we'd been talking about, I look up at him.

Maddox sighs. "So pretty. So forgetful."

That makes me narrow my eyes at him.

He reaches past me, tapping Chelsea on the shoulder.

"What?" She turns away from her friends to face us.

"Smidge, change spots with Hannah."

Chelsea looks around me at the big man. "Why?"

He pulls his arm back from around me and wedges it down his side, which shoves me over into Chelsea's space. "Because I'm a monster and you're Smidge, and then I can take up all the space you don't use."

Chelsea snorts, then taps her finger to her chin. "What do I get out of it?"

I open my mouth to tell her blackmail isn't nice, but Maddox answers first.

"What do you want?"

"Mini donuts." Her eyes widen as she says it.

We purposely ate lunch at home before Maddox picked us up so we wouldn't have to spend a fortune buying food here. But mini donuts do sound amazing.

"Anything else?"

I look at Maddox. "You're not really good at negotiating, are you?"

"I plan to eat half the donuts myself." He shrugs.

Chelsea thinks. "A slushie?"

Maddox looks at me. "How about you, Auntie?"

Auntie.

"Um..." *Why does that sound so dirty when he says it?* "A slushie sounds good."

"'Kay." Maddox wedges himself up to standing, then points at Chelsea. "Smidge, you're with me."

I start to stand, but Maddox shakes his head. "We got this."

Hesitating, I look at him, then over at Chelsea.

They get along — that's clear to see. But I don't want either of them to feel like they have to spend time together if they don't want to.

But then Chelsea climbs over my legs to get out, zero hesitation on her face as she points to the cupholder in front of her seat. "I left my water."

I look where she's pointing, and when I turn back, they've already started up the stairs.

I blow out a breath and slump back into my seat.

Before I can overthink *everything*, there's a soft tap on my shoulder.

I expect to see a mom when I turn, but it's a boy about Chelsea's age.

He's leaned so far forward it's a miracle he's still on his seat at all. "My dad wants to know if that's Mad Dog Maddox."

I glance at the man sitting next to the kid.

He tugs on his son's shirt. "You're such a snitch."

The kid ignores his dad. "It's him though, isn't it?"

Even though it's just these two talking to me, I can feel several people waiting for my answer.

I nod my head.

"I knew it!" The kid sits back, triumphant.

It's the dad's turn to lean forward. "Do you think it'd be okay if we took a picture with him?"

"Uh." I look around, taking in all the stares. "I don't think he'd mind. But... maybe after the game?"

The dad nods. "Totally, that'd be cool."

His son elbows him. "We should've worn our Biters jerseys."

The dad sits back. "Well, you should've told me your class-mate's dad was Maddox Lovelace."

"I didn't know!"

Oh boy. That's not a rumor I need going around Chelsea's school.

"Um." I cut into their conversation. "Maddox isn't her dad. He's, uh, my boyfriend."

EIGHTY
MADDOX

At the top of the stairs, Chelsea pauses. "Which way?"

I stop behind her. "Not sure."

"Well, look." She gestures around. "You can see over everyone, right?"

"Fair point." I set my hand on the top of her head so I don't lose her and step us out into the center of the main walkway.

I look one way, then the other. "It might be —" I cut myself off. "Never mind, I see it."

"Told ya," Chelsea singsongs.

Keeping her in front of me, we make our way down to the donut stand.

The line is long, snaking along the wall, so we step up and take our place at the end.

"You been keeping yourself busy?" I ask Chelsea. "Learn any new ways to cheat at poker?"

She slowly turns around to look up at me. "You and I both know I didn't have to cheat."

"Says you."

She lifts a brow. "I'm happy for a rematch. But maybe you want to practice more first."

"Hmm. Maybe I should get some cheats — I mean lessons — from whoever taught you."

"You couldn't afford them."

Chelsea's comeback makes me snort. "That so? Who was it, a pro?"

"Nah, just some old lady who used to live next door. I didn't get really good until I started playing online. But after I won five hundred bucks one time, Aunt Hannah flipped out and told me I couldn't play anymore."

"Five hundred? Damn."

"I know, right?"

"When you're old enough for the Vegas casinos, I'll get you into one of their poker tourneys."

Her eyes light up. "Really?"

"Really." This kid is gonna steal someone's savings out from under them. And I want to be there to witness it.

We shuffle forward in line.

Someone's fallen popcorn crunches under my tennis shoes, and when I glance down, I notice the laces on my left shoe are coming undone.

I make sure there's enough room between me and the family in line behind us, then I crouch down and start retying my laces.

"What are you doing?" Chelsea snaps.

Her tone is surprisingly angry, so I jerk my head up, but she's not talking to me. Instead, she's talking to some teenage punk that just stepped in front of her in line.

The boy shrugs. "Cutting."

Oh, hell no.

"Go to the back of the line, Ken."

Ken? What fucking parent named their kid Ken?

"No," the little shit answers with his back to Chelsea.

I rise to my full height.

"I'm telling you for the last time," Chelsea grits out.

Her tone is full of derision, and it makes me proud as hell.

"Or what?" Ken says in a stupid tone as he starts to turn around. "You gonna make me?"

I move so I'm next to Smidge and cross my arms. Shoulders back. Mad Dog face in place.

"No," Chelsea snarks. "But he will."

Ken opens his dumb mouth, but he doesn't say anything. He just stares up at me, with his eyes bugging out of his head.

Beside me, Chelsea shifts her stance, and I'm sure it's full of attitude.

Ken starts to move his attention back to Chelsea.

"Back of the line, Ken." I use my deepest voice before he can say something to Smidge that will piss me all the way off.

The teen makes a face like he's fighting with himself whether to say something shitty or not, and apparently, the smart half wins because he stomps off.

We're silent for a moment before I look down at Chelsea. "So, he kinda sucks."

"Oh my god, that was the best thing ever!" She cackles. "I need to bring you to school with me."

I scowl. "Are you getting bullied?"

She waves that off as we move ahead in the line. "What? No. But some boys are just annoying."

I mentally double down on Ruth's *no dating until thirty-five* rule. "Boys are the worst. Don't trust any of them."

"Duh."

I accept that was an obvious statement.

"Well, if anyone is *extra* annoying, tell me."

"Yeah, sure." It's a blow-off statement if I've ever heard one. "What should we get?"

We're close enough to read the menu now, and while I read the options, I wonder if there's a career day or something I could go to at Chelsea's school for the sole purpose of putting the fear of Mad Dog into the hearts of any boy who might dream of even talking to her.

When it's our turn, we decide on the bucket.

I make Chelsea carry it so I'm not tempted to eat them by the handful, then guide her back the way we came.

As we walk away, Ken shouts, "The Biters suck!"

Chelsea spins around, looking ready to throw down, and before I can stop her, she shouts back, "Your science project sucked!"

A laugh barks out of me, but I try to cover it with a cough.

"Smidge, that wasn't nice." It's hard to chastise her when I'm still trying not to laugh, and now I appreciate all the times I've witnessed Hannah in this same position even more.

"He deserved it."

"I trust your judgment." I hold my hand out. "Give me a donut, and I'll pretend I didn't hear you insulting that kid's schoolwork."

Chelsea holds up the bucket.

I take two and shove them both in my mouth.

When I look down, Chelsea is making a face at me.

"What?" I ask, mouth still full.

"Are you gonna marry Aunt Hannah?"

I swallow the rest of my donut.

I wasn't expecting her to ask that. But a direct question deserves a direct answer. "I'd like to. You okay with that?"

She purses her lips, then shrugs. "Yeah. You're alright."

Her easy acceptance warms my whole damn soul.

"Stop it." I hunch my shoulders. "You're gonna make me blush."

Smidge shakes her head. "I take it back. You're a dork."

I mock gasp. "You wound me."

Instead of apologizing, she holds up the donuts, and I take two more.

This kid gets me.

Then I spot the perfect thing.

"Hold up." I grip her sleeve, pulling her off to the side. "One more stop before the slushies."

EIGHTY-ONE

HANNAH

The last note of the national anthem ends, and I'm about ready
to send out a search party for Maddox and Chelsea.

I've been so focused on waiting for them to get back — and
fending off questions about Maddox — that I didn't even pay
attention to what team we're playing against.

"Who are we playing?" I ask the mom seated next to me
since I've already moved into Chelsea's seat — thinking she and
Maddox would've been back by now.

"Um." Her brows furrow.

The boy on the other side of her points to the player getting
ready to bat. "The Windy City Warriors."

His mom nods. "That's right."

Then her gaze moves past me, and from the way her eyes
widen, I know they're back.

But even knowing that, I'm not prepared for what I see
when I turn my head.

"What are you wearing?" I ask through a laugh.

Maddox tilts his head. "What do you mean?"

I look between him and Chelsea, but they both keep

straight faces. Though I can't see their eyes, so maybe they're crinkled with humor.

I hold out my hand. "Give me my slushie, you goofballs."

Maddox nudges Chelsea to scoot into the row first, with her large slushie in one hand and a bucket of donuts in the other.

I peek into the bucket. "Hope you got a discount."

Chelsea plops into the seat. "Yeah, it's called the Maddox discount, where he eats eight at a time."

"It was two at a time," Maddox replies as he wedges himself back into the seat at the end of the row. "And I told you to keep them away from me."

"Uh-huh, so it's my fault."

I assume she's rolling her eyes.

Maddox balances the drink tray on his lap and pulls my slushie free, handing it across Chelsea.

"Thanks," I tell him and take a sip of the cherry ice. "We really not talking about the accessories?"

Maddox tips his head toward the field. "Game is starting."

Sighing, I give up and steal a donut from Chelsea.

But even as I watch the first round of pitches, I keep looking over at the oddball pair next to me.

The twelve-year-old girl and the massive man, sitting side by side, wearing matching gaudy plastic necklaces, each bead about the size of a golf ball, and printed to look like a baseball. But it's the glasses that are the most absurd. The plastic rims look snug on Maddox but oversized on Chelsea, but it's not the fit that's ridiculous. It's the lenses. Like the beads, the image of a baseball is printed onto them.

It's silly. And unnecessary. And the sight of these two matching makes me want to cry.

EIGHTY-TWO
MADDOX

As the teams switch places on the field, I lower my glasses down my nose so I can look over at Hannah.

We've been watching the game, sure, but she's still been awfully quiet.

She notices me and turns her head.

"Everything okay?" I ask quietly, but since Chelsea is between us, it's not private.

Hannah nods. "I'm really good."

I watch her face for any signs of unease but don't find any. "If you're feeling left out about the necklaces, I can go get you one."

"I'm pretty jealous, but I'll survive." She gestures to her eyes. "It's a good disguise."

I nod. "And they look cool."

That gets me a laugh. "Keep telling yourself that."

Hannah's eyes dart to the row behind us, then she leans toward me.

I nudge Chelsea. "Smidge, scoot up a smidge."

She huffs but slides forward on her seat so Hannah and I can lean together behind her.

We keep our faces turned forward, but it's obvious we're talking.

"I told the guys behind us that you'd take a photo with them after the game," she whispers.

"Okay," I whisper back.

"And, um, I told them you were my boyfriend," she says nervously. "It's just that they thought you were her dad and I panicked and I —"

I turn my head so I can press my lips to Hannah's temple.

She stops talking.

"Little Bunny," I whisper against her ear, making sure she hears me. "I am your boyfriend. And I'm the last one you'll ever have."

"Hannah, hold the door!"

I almost groan out loud at the sound of Brandon's voice because, really, I don't want to hold the door open for him. But I do because even *he* can't ruin the overall feeling of happiness that has settled over me.

"Thanks," Brandon heaves the word like he just finished a 5K.

"No problem" is what I say, but "Go away" is what I think.

Donut Guy is at his table, and Roberts is filling up his coffee thermos as we cross the break room.

I shift my container of leftover casserole into my left hand and pull the fridge open with my right.

Once the door is already open, Brandon — who is now completely crowding my personal space — pulls the door open farther so he can grab one of his nasty energy drinks from the shelf in the door.

Yeah, please, barge right in.

As I reach to put my food on the shelf, there's already a glass container in the spot I usually put my lunch.

And then I freeze. Because there's a Post-it, with my name on it, stuck to the lid of the container in the fridge.

Brandon finally steps back, and I shift closer to look through the clear sides of the dish.

I swallow and set my casserole on top of the dish containing the lemon butter noodles and grilled chicken.

Last night, Maddox and I sat on a video call for an hour while he grilled chicken breasts and made a batch of the same lemony pasta he cooked for our movie date.

It's become our evening norm.

My family tends to eat earlier than he does, so after I'm done with dinner, Maddox calls, and I lounge while he cooks and eats his dinner.

It's... God, it's everything.

It's the phone calls we missed.

It's the evening version of the long-distance relationship we weren't allowed to try.

It's a way to spend time together, to talk, without being interrupted by the overwhelming need to touch each other.

It's torture. And it's exactly what I need.

"Forget your food from last week?" Brandon asks from next to me.

I blink and shut the fridge door. "Yeah. Threw me off for a second," I joke.

Brandon looks at the fridge, then back to me, like he's sensing the lie.

I move around him to the mug cupboard and take my time selecting one.

My call with Maddox last night made me forget all about my promise to check on my job applications. Which was foolish, because I need to get out of here so we can properly date each other.

I'm the last one you'll ever have.

Maddox knows all the right things to say.

And I could cry just from picturing him with Chelsea this past weekend, in their glasses, shit talking some kid's science fair project the whole ride home from the game.

It was literally the second time they met, and they acted like —

I pull down the handmade yellow mug Maddox used the time he made me coffee.

They acted like family.

If anyone can break the curse, it's gotta be him.

"You're acting weird." Brandon is back at my side. "Are you alright?"

Oh my god, go away.

"Just haven't had my coffee yet," I lie, since I had a cup at home this morning.

He hums and leans against the counter. The opposite of leaving.

"Do anything fun this weekend?" Brandon asks.

"Yeah, I went to a baseball game."

"The Kids game?"

I nod.

"Didn't we lose?" he asks, like that makes the difference on enjoying a game or not.

I shrug. "It was still a fun time."

He's quiet for a second as I pour my coffee.

"Who'd you go with?"

I pause as I put the pot back in its place.

It's not like it's *that* weird of a question. But it's kinda weird. Though it gives me an opportunity to try and set some boundaries.

"Chelsea and I went with a bunch of people from her school." I pull a spoon out of the drawer. "And my boyfriend came with us."

"You have a boyfriend?" Brandon's whole body shifts back like I just told him I'm a werewolf.

"Hannah." A voice richer than Brandon's speaks from behind me.

I turn to face the boyfriend in question.

"Morning," I say, more softly than I mean to.

Maddox holds up the carton of half-and-half I forgot to take out of the fridge when I put my lunch in there.

"Need this?"

I take it from him, trying not to smile too hard over the creamer. "Thanks."

Turning back to the counter, I pour some into my mug, then stir the contents around.

Brandon is standing there, looking back and forth between us. But instead of addressing him, Maddox holds his hand out to take the creamer back.

"I got that."

Since I don't really want to have to shuffle between him and Brandon, I hand Maddox the carton.

He inclines his head. "Have a nice morning."

"You too." I pick up my coffee, biting down on my lip.

I'm walking away when Maddox speaks again.

"Brandon. A word."

EIGHTY-FOUR
MADDOX

Brandon stops after one step, and I don't move, forcing him to turn toward me and away from Hannah.

I wasn't about to have him watch her walk away in that fucking dress.

He's not looking at *my girlfriend*.

"Yeah?" His tone is awfully short, considering he's talking to the owner of the company.

I wait a heartbeat longer than comfortable before I talk. "Darren in technical needs a pair of eyes from someone in sales to look at some tech sheets."

"Oh, I don't —" he starts.

But this isn't a democracy.

"He asked for you by name." Actually, what Darren said was *"You should make that Brandon guy do it, he always has an opinion anyway."* But his name was mentioned. "Shouldn't take up too much time." I turn and pull a mug from the cupboard.

Brandon mumbles an agreement before leaving.

I add sugar to my coffee and put Hannah's creamer away.

When I'm stepping away from the counter with my mug in hand, Donut Man lifts his head.

"Nice moves."

My steps slow. "What's that?"

The older guy tips his head toward the coffee maker. "Slick way of getting him away from your girl."

With no one else in here to see, I smirk. "I thought so."

EIGHTY-FIVE
HANNAH

A calendar invite dings on my computer.

I click on it and have to read the invite twice. Because it's from Maddox.

For two o'clock. In his office. Apparently to discuss Q4 projections.

I look at the clock.

It's one forty-five.

My phone vibrates on the desk, and I pick it up.

BB Wolf: Don't be late.

EIGHTY-SIX
MADDOX

"Ah, Hannah, just on time." I greet her with my typical corporate tone. "Come on in."

The last part is unnecessary since she's already crossing the threshold, but it's my standard greeting.

I shouldn't have asked her to come. Shouldn't have sent the calendar invite, but this weekend was PG, and that dress she's wearing is giving me R-rated thoughts.

Her hips sway as she walks toward the visitor's chair across from my desk, causing her skirt to dance around her knees.

It's not a provocative dress, not by any typical standard. But on her? Knowing what her soft skin feels like underneath...

I work my jaw.

The gray material looks stretchy, and it's pulled deliciously across her chest in a modest enough neckline. But her tits. Goddamn those tits. If I was still in college and had a few beers, I would one thousand percent motorboat them. But since I'm mature now, I just want to suck on them.

The sleeves are fitted and stop at her elbows, more modesty.

And below her breasts, the material flares out.

It shouldn't be this sexy.

Well, *it* isn't.

She's sexy. No matter what she wears. It just so happens that this particular choice gives me all sorts of ideas.

Hannah stops on the other side of the desk from me. "I brought those files you wanted."

She holds up another plain folder, and with her back to the door, holding one corner with two fingers, she lets the folder flop open.

Nothing falls out.

But she's written something inside.

You're bad.

"Have a seat." I grin at her as I stand. "You're exactly right." I talk in my normal volume as I cross to my door. "The expenses for last quarter were a little high, but that was to be expected with the merger." I grip the door handle and casually push it shut. "I want to look closely at the next step." As the door clicks shut, I depress the button in the center of the handle, locking it.

I turn back to face Hannah.

She's sitting in the chair, angled so she can see me.

"That's not where I want you to sit."

Her chest rises with an inhale. "Maddox —"

I shake my head as I start toward her. "It's Mr. Lovelace until I open that door. Now stand up."

EIGHTY-SEVEN
HANNAH

My heart is racing.

I was almost certain he called me in here for sex, was prepared for it. But I should know better. I'm never prepared for Maddox.

My legs feel unsteady as I stand. "Where would you like me, Mr. Lovelace?"

A low sound comes out of his chest.

He looks how he always does in the office. Button-down shirt tucked into nice pants. No tie. Sleeves rolled up. But with the way he's stalking toward me, he looks like someone else.

"On the desk, Miss Utley." His command lacks volume, not intensity.

I back away from him until my butt bumps into the front edge of his desk.

A glance behind me shows that he's already cleared off the surface.

Such a clever boy.

I reach my hands down to boost myself up, but I'm not fast enough for Maddox.

He hooks his hands under my arms and lifts me until I'm sitting on his desk.

The loose skirt of my dress allows me to spread my knees, and Maddox steps between my thighs.

"About those projections..." I whisper, well aware we need to be very quiet.

Maddox presses his hand to my chest, his warm palm against my flushed skin. "It's gonna be a hard start." He slides his hand up until he's gently holding the front of my throat. "And we'll have to stay under the radar." His other hand starts at my knee, sliding up underneath my dress. "But, it'll probably go quick."

I lean forward. Just a little. But it's enough to put a little pressure on my throat.

And I like it.

Maddox had been looking down at his hand under my dress, but the moan I tried to stifle must have vibrated against his palm, because his eyes snap up to mine.

"You're a bad girl, Miss Utley." A finger traces over my panties, right over my slit. "Should we find out how bad?"

Holy Jesus.

I nod. And my chin automatically lifts for a kiss.

Maddox leans down, his mouth an inch away from mine. "No kissing. Or else your lips will get all swollen and red, and everyone will know."

His lips brush against mine with every word, then he pulls back.

And kneels down.

"Lie back." His whisper sends a shiver racing down my spine straight to my clit.

Doing as I'm told, I lower myself until I'm lying back across the desk.

Maddox grips my legs and adjusts them until they're

settled over his shoulders. Then, with his arms hooked up and around my thighs, he pulls me to the edge of the desk.

My skirt is yanked up, and he leaves it bunched on top of my stomach.

I expect him to tell me to lift my hips so he can pull my underwear off, but he tugs them aside, keeping them on while exposing my core.

"Hmm, what's this, Miss Utley?" I can feel his exhaled words against my bare flesh.

He slides his finger against my entrance, up the length of me, and I press a hand over my mouth to keep from gasping out loud.

"Did you come into your boss's office with a dripping pussy?" He drags his finger back down. "Does that seem like good behavior or bad behavior?"

Without waiting for an answer, Maddox closes his mouth over my clit and sucks.

My back arches, and my feet hook together behind Maddox's head while I try not to make a sound.

I close my eyes, and I drop my arm across my face.

Maddox doesn't stop.

His tongue works up and down my slit, pushing deeper and deeper until he's licking inside me.

Pressure is applied to my clit, and I imagine it's his thumb pressing against me.

I want to scream. I want to rip all the clothes from my body.

I want —

A finger pushes into me, and I clench.

Maddox moans against me.

His tongue licks again. And again.

Heat fills my limbs, and I feel the need to release rapidly building inside me.

He pushes his finger deeper and closes his lips around my clit.

Maddox sucks on the little bundle of nerves as the tip of his tongue rubs it.

"M —" I drop my hand from my mouth. "Mr. Lovelace, I'm so close." My words are soft pants into the silent room.

His lips release my clit so he can flatten his tongue against me for one last swipe.

Maddox shifts, and I unhook my feet from around his neck as I lift my arm over my eyes.

Big hands grip the back of my knees, and he pushes them up, keeping me exposed and making room for him to stand.

I hook my hands behind my knees to keep them up.

Maddox pulls a silk handkerchief out of his pocket and rubs it across his mouth and chin before dropping it on the desk next to my hip.

No way should that be so sexy.

With his eyes on mine, he undoes his belt and pants, slowly and quietly lowering the zipper.

When he gets his cock out, I let my eyes drop.

Even his dick is handsome.

Gripping the base of his dick in one hand, Maddox pulls my panties to the side again.

"I'm going to put my cock in you now, Miss Utley. Are you ready?"

I blink, wanting to watch him during this part, and whisper, "I'm ready for you, Mr. Lovelace."

NINETY-ONE

HANNAH

My core squeezes.

Having just the tip of Maddox inside me as I come is such a different sensation.

It's intense. Open.

And I ride out the end of my orgasm, watching him tense, then hunch as he reaches the end of his orgasm.

His eyes blink like he's trying to focus his vision. And I know the feeling.

Maddox steadies himself, then reaches to the side and picks up his discarded handkerchief.

Beyond being embarrassed, I keep my legs spread and let him clean up the mess he created.

When he's done, he pulls my damp panties back into place and balls up the silk kerchief. With his free hand, he grips mine and helps me sit up.

We're still breathing heavily, but I have to smile up at him. "We really can't keep doing this, Mr. Lovelace. We're gonna get caught."

He gives me that grin I adore. "This is the price you pay for sleeping in your own bed all weekend."

Maddox presses a quick kiss to my lips, then moves away.

I slip off the desk and straighten my dress, ignoring the feeling between my thighs.

Before coming in here, I took off the little shorts I always wear under this dress. So when I get back to my office, I'll hide these panties in my garbage and put the shorts back on instead.

Maddox reappears in front of me with two bottles of water.

He holds one out. "There's still time left in our meeting. Sit down and drink."

I open the bottle. "So bossy."

He smirks, opening his own. "Just trying to get that *freshly fucked* look off your face. But if you want to go out now..."

I lift the bottle and take a drink. "Having a reason doesn't make you less bossy."

Maddox chuckles and takes a big swallow.

Sighing, I drop back into the visitor's chair. "I know my mom and Chelsea wouldn't care if I spent the occasional night at your place. I just feel so guilty any time I leave them."

It's nothing but the truth, and it's been on my mind since the one night I did sleep over.

Maddox turns the other visitor's chair toward me and lowers himself into it. Then he hooks his foot around the leg of my chair, turning it until we're facing each other.

"I don't ever want to make you feel guilty, Hannah." He leans in, placing his hand on my thigh. "And I promise I'll never make you choose between me or them." His mouth pulls into a soft smile.

"I know you wouldn't, and that's —" I stop.

That's why I love you.

He squeezes my leg. "I don't want to rush you."

A half-broken laugh falls out of me.

I set my hand on his. "You're hardly rushing me, Maddox. If it were up to me, and the logistics weren't so complicated, I'd spend every night sharing a bed with you."

As soon as I say it, it feels like too much. But his unwavering grip on me stops the nerves from forming.

"We'll get those logistics figured out, Little Bunny. And until then" — he smirks — "we just have to be creative."

NINETY-TWO
HANNAH

With my soiled undies hidden inside my purse — because I couldn't bring myself to leave them in my office trash can — I climb the steps and unlock the front door.

I can hear Christmas music coming from the kitchen, and the sound of it makes me smile.

The choice of genre might seem weird to anyone else, but it's Mom's tradition to listen to holiday music anytime she bakes cookies. Which is why, even though I should really go take a shower, I follow the scent of vanilla and browned butter across the house.

"What're you..." I trail off as I cross the threshold into the small kitchen and blink at their outfits. "What are you wearing?"

Chelsea and Mom look up at the same time, then simultaneously drop their attention back to the little island where they are...

I move closer.

Oh.

Okay, sure. This is normal.

Just my family making sugar cookies shaped like little football jerseys. Decorating them with red and yellow frosting to mimic the colors of the Biters. And at least three have the number ninety-nine piped on with white icing.

Ninety-nine. Maddox's number.

I reach out and touch the corner of one.

"Maddox had them sent over," Chelsea tells me as she squeezes her piping bag.

"The cookies?" I ask, confused.

"Huh?" Chelsea glances up at me like I'm crazy. "No, we made these." She gestures to the two dozen jersey cookies. "We used Grandma's Christmas sweater cookie cutter."

"That's, uh, clever." I have no clue what is going on or why they're pretending this isn't completely bonkers. "Do the cookies have something to do with all the..." I wave my hand at them. "Outfits."

Chelsea makes a sound, but Mom answers. "Aren't they nice?" Mom holds her arms out and twists side to side. "Chelsea said we should bake something as a thank-you, and then when we came across the sweater cutter, well, an idea was born."

I widen my eyes. "Will someone just tell me what the hell is going on?"

"Oh hush, we're trying to concentrate." Mom waves me off. "Yours is on the dining table."

I look between Mom and my niece, taking in the real human-sized Minnesota Biters jerseys they're wearing. And I take in the baseball hat on Chelsea's head with the embroidered mosquito mascot. And the red, yellow, and white pompom hat on Mom's head.

"What —"

Mom cuts me off. "Go open your gift."

I puff my cheeks out and spin around. "Fine."

Obviously, Maddox was involved in whatever this is. At this point, I don't even know why I'm surprised by anything he does.

Stopping in front of the table, I look at the white box sitting on the surface. My name is printed on a small sticker stuck to the corner of the box.

There are two empty boxes on the other side of the table, lids tossed carelessly to the side. But I lift the lid off my box slowly.

A small card sits on top of the tissue-wrapped interior.

I take it out.

My Little Bunny,

I won't have my girl (or her family) wearing any number but mine.

And to replace what was... lost.

Love,

Your Big Bad Wolf

Feeling unsteady, I set the card aside.

Love.

My fingers tremble as I peel the tissue paper back. A jersey just like the one Mom and Chelsea are wearing is folded inside.

The material is thick, the stitching is pristine, and when I hold it up, I can tell he got the perfect size.

Turning it over, I look at his name. *Lovelace.*

How many times did I dream of wearing this?

How many times did I imagine in my mind that we were madly in love, and I was at his game, in the stands, wearing this exact jersey?

I drape the jersey over the back of the chair and pull the next item out of the box.

My throat tightens.

It's not a hat.

And it's not from the Biters.

It's a gray zip-up hoodie. With the HOP University logo high on the chest, over the heart.

A replica of the one I kept from him.

The one I burned.

And it doesn't matter that the house is warm from all the baking, I unzip it and shove my arms inside the sleeves.

It's sized for Maddox, not for me.

And dammit.

I love him.

Tears well in my eyes, and I pull the sides of the sweatshirt across each other, wrapping the material around my body.

I love this man.

The one who gives my niece nicknames.

The one who makes me dinner and fulfills old promises.

The man who takes up just as much space in my heart as he does in real life.

I love him.

And I don't really know what to do about that.

"Show us what you got," Mom calls from the kitchen.

My breath hitches. Mom is one of the two reasons why I don't know what to do.

"Yeah, come on. I wanna show you this cookie," Chelsea, the other reason, shouts even though we're only ten feet away.

I wipe at my eyes.

Maddox told me he wouldn't ask me to choose between him and them, but ultimately, won't it come down to that? Or does he plan to wait six years until Chelsea goes to college before we take our relationship to the next level? And even then, I can't just leave my mom behind. We've been living together for my thirty-five years of existence.

She's recovered, been better for a long time, and could physically live on her own. But could I really leave her at the same time Chelsea leaves?

Would I want to?

I blink up at the ceiling.

Am I seriously crying over the idea that I might not live with my mom for the rest of my mortal life?

What is wrong with me?

Shaking my head, I sniff a few times and dab at my eyes with the edge of my hoodie sleeve. Then I step back into the kitchen.

"Ooh, that's cute." Mom smiles at the blue and black logo on my hoodie. "It's like the one you lost."

Yep, lost it at that park I never went to.

Chelsea scrunches up her face. "That's... nice."

"It is." I run my palms down the fabric. "I got a jersey too, if that's more impressive."

She nods.

"Speaking of, should you two really be wearing those while baking?" I can't help but ask. "I don't exactly know how to wash that material."

Mom waves off my concern with a bag of icing. "Maddox told us not to baby them."

It takes a second for that sentence to sink in.

"Maddox... told you," I repeat slowly.

"Mm-hmm." Mom leans back over the counter to keep decorating a cookie. "And we figured you could bring them to dinner as the dessert."

It feels like I just sat down halfway through a movie I've never heard of.

"Look at this one." Chelsea pushes a cookie toward me.

"What dinner?" I ask Mom, confused, as I move closer to the counter.

"The one tomorrow. Maddox will call you." Her answer doesn't make any more sense than her previous statements.

I stare at Mom, but she isn't paying attention to me.

What in the hell is she talking about?

"Aunt Hannah." Chelsea's impatient tone forces my gaze back down.

"Sorry." I turn the cookie so it's facing me.

Smidge is written across it.

And I die.

I've lost the battle against reality.

I'm no longer of this world.

I'm just a ghost floating away.

I'm dead.

"Uh, Grandma, what's wrong with her?" Chelsea says from somewhere in the afterlife.

"She's just having a moment," Mom replies.

I stare at the counter. The cookies. The ones with ninety-nine on them. The ones with hearts. The ones with footballs. The one that says *Smidge*. The one that says... I tilt my head. Is that G. Ma?

Mom's phone rings, and she answers. "Hello, Maddy."

I blink.

Maddy?

"Yes, she's here." Mom nods. "Yeah. Uh-huh. No. I think she's just a little overwhelmed. Having a bit of an episode."

"Mom," I sigh.

She glances at me but keeps talking into the phone. "Yep. She's wearing the hoodie. Hmm, I don't know how to do that."

"Mom." I try again. "Are you talking to Maddox?"

She turns her head away from me.

I pick up one of the jersey cookies and bite the sleeve off.

It's good. Very vanilla-y.

"Okay. Okay. Alright, I'll look," Mom says to *Maddox* before she pulls the phone away from her ear and taps the screen. "Is it working?"

"Yep, I can see you." A male voice I know too well sounds through the speaker of Mom's phone.

Mom lets out a sound of enjoyment as she holds the phone out, letting us all see Maddox's handsome face on the screen.

"Hey, Smidge." He greets Chelsea.

"Hey." She only spares the phone a glance before going back to decorating the next cookie.

"Let me see the sweatshirt," he says to my mom.

She tries to hold it at the right angle but gives up and hands me the phone. "You can do it."

Taking it, I walk out of the kitchen and sink into one of the dining chairs.

Resting my elbow on the table, I hold the phone up so I'm looking into Maddox's kind eyes.

"Hey, Bunny."

I shake my head. Then I shake my head again. And finally, a stupid smile wins out, pulling across my features. "What is wrong with you?"

He presses a hand to his chest. "Moi?"

"No." I shake my head. "You do not get to be handsome, sweet, *and* speak French."

He chuckles. "If it makes you feel better, my command of the French language is extremely limited."

"It helps."

I took French for a few years back in high school, and the idea of Maddox speaking it to me is too much.

Maddox smirks. "So... does the fact that you're already wearing the hoodie mean you don't plan to burn it?"

I lift a shoulder. "Only time will tell."

"Fair. Reserve the right of destruction."

I look at his familiar features. "You didn't need to do it, ya know?"

"The hoodie?"

"The hoodie. The jerseys. The hats. Any of it." I need him to understand. "We don't need you to buy us things. We like you already."

His smile softens. "I know, Bunny. But thank you for saying it."

"I like gifts!" Chelsea shouts from the kitchen, proving she's eavesdropping.

"Tell her she's my favorite."

"I will not," I reply.

You're my favorite he mouths.

I press my lips together.

He tips his head down. "Does the jersey fit too?"

"Haven't tried it on yet." The phone in my hand dings loudly with a notification, reminding me it's Mom's phone. "Why are we talking on my mom's phone?"

"Because you weren't answering yours."

"And when did you and my mom exchange numbers?"

"When I dropped off the gifts."

I narrow my gaze. "And when did you drop off the gifts?"

"Over lunch."

"So, you were here before our... meeting, and you didn't mention it?"

Maddox shrugs. "We had to stay on topic."

"Stay... on topic."

"Speaking of lunch." He brushes past the whole *him stopping over here* thing. "I'd like you to join me for dinner tomorrow."

My lips purse. "What sort of dinner?"

NINETY-THREE
MADDOX

I push away from the side of the building.

Hannah just climbed out of the back seat of an Uber, and she looks so fucking fuckable I have to shove my hand in my pocket and pinch my thigh so I don't pop a boner.

Her heels click against the sidewalk as she walks toward me, and the setting sun bathes her in a golden glow.

Her hair is down, curled into waves, and I want to look at her beautiful face, but my eyes are too focused everywhere else.

I don't know what material her top is made of, but it looks soft. The neckline plunges between her glorious breasts, and the hem is tucked into fitted navy pants that hug her all the way down to her ankles.

I smooth my hands down my black Henley, feeling suddenly underdressed in my jeans.

She has a large purse hanging from one hand, so she lifts the other and wiggles her fingers at me.

I stride toward her.

"Little Bunny," I growl, wanting nothing more than to eat her up.

Wanting to touch her.

I'm one step away when I remember we're not at work.

I can touch her.

I don't have to hold back.

When she's within reaching distance, I grip her hip with one hand and slide the other around the side of her neck until my fingers are buried in the hair at the back of her head. And I kiss her.

I kiss my girl.

My lips on hers.

My mouth moving against hers.

My tongue pushing between her lips. Her opening to me.

God, I needed this.

Hands flatten against my chest, and her fingers curl, digging her nails into my muscles.

She moans into me.

And I feel my cock start to harden.

"Fuck, Babe," I breathe against her mouth. "We gotta stop."

Her lips curl into a smile against mine. "You started it."

"Hmm. We could finish in my car," I offer.

She pushes against me with her palms, and I finally take a step back.

"Maddox Lovelace, you told me you were taking me to dinner." She straightens her shirt. "And I didn't go through all the stress of getting ready to meet your best friend and brother just for you to change the plan."

I brush my thumb across her cheek. "Don't be nervous. They're gonna love you."

As much as I do. I think it but don't say it.

I want to tell her. But I just have a few more things to do first.

"Let's go." I hold my hand out for her to take. "I sent Max in already to get our table."

Hannah slides her hand into mine, and I walk us toward the restaurant's entrance.

It's a nice place, great food, moody atmosphere, and hipster enough that even if the clientele recognized me or Waller, or potentially Max, they'd be *too cool* to approach us. The restaurant has just the right level of douchebag vibes for us to be left alone.

Keeping my hold of Hannah's hand, I pull open the door and guide her in before me. There's a second door, and we have to shift around for me to open it again, but I can feel the nerves radiating off my girl, and I'm not letting her go.

"Good evening." The hostess greets us.

"Hello." Hannah's voice is a little more timid than I'm used to hearing, so I squeeze her hand.

"We're meeting —" I start, then spot Max. "I see our table."

"Go right ahead." The hostess smiles, and we step past.

My brother has been spending his summer down in Arizona but flew back for a visit.

I would have invited my parents along, let everyone meet Hannah at the same time, but they're at some friend's birthday tonight. So it's just us, my little brother and Waller.

Hannah peeks out from behind me to look at the table we're approaching. "I thought you said two people?" she whispers.

I stop at the table, replying loud enough for the guys to hear. "I did say we were meeting two people."

NINETY-FOUR
HANNAH

Maddox shakes the hand of the guy nearest him, and they clap each other on the backs in that way men do. "I was just thinking about you the other day."

"Either you missed me, or someone pissed you off." The man chuckles.

With Maddox no longer holding my hand, I twist my fingers together in front of me and keep my focus on the men hugging because I don't want to have to introduce myself to the other guys.

"Tony." Maddox pulls away and lifts his hand to my back, pulling me next to him. "This is my girl, Hannah. Hannah, this is Tony Stoleman."

I try for a relaxed smile as I shake his hand. "Nice to meet you."

Tony is handsome, nearly as tall as Maddox, with a dimple in his cheek and hair almost as dark as Maddox's. But his energy is a little... different. Kind of intense.

"When I heard our guy was bringing *the* Hannah Utley to

dinner, I had to crash." He winks at me. "Hope you don't mind."

The Hannah Utley?

"And this" — Maddox raises his voice as he pulls my hand free from Tony's grip — "is my friend Nate Waller. But we just call him Waller."

"Hi, Hannah." The man grins, and good grief, he's just as handsome as the other guy, only he has a way lighter feel about him.

From the opposite side of the round table, Waller starts to reach across. But before I can move, Maddox slaps Waller's hand away. "You don't all need to fucking touch her."

Waller holds his hands up and sits back down in his chair.

Maddox shifts me to his other side, so I'm between him and the last man.

This one is younger than the rest, not much over twenty, with hair and eyes that can only belong to a Lovelace.

"You must be Max. I've heard lots of good things," I tell Maddox's little brother.

"Same. Maddox doesn't shut up about you." He smiles, not moving to stand or shake my hand, just holding his hand up in greeting.

I wave back, feeling a little more at ease.

Maddox pulls out the chair next to Max and gestures for me to take it.

I had to bring my bulky purse, the only one that can fit a giant Tupperware inside it, so I shove the bag under my chair.

Maddox sits next to me, putting me between the Lovelace brothers. Tony and Waller grin at us from the other side.

The round table means it's easier to see everyone, but it also feels like everyone is staring at me.

NINETY-FIVE
NATE WALLER

Maddox lounges back, putting his arm around the top of Hannah's chair.

In the times we've talked since I first found out she was working for him, he's been nothing shy of infatuated. But since I know the history, I was skeptical.

Maddox was the one who spent fucking years talking about her — the girl who disappeared after his *night in the library*. So it's not my fault for not readily believing they were suddenly a happy couple.

But ten minutes of being at the same table and I can tell it's not fake.

His fingers skim across her shoulder.

Her hand reaches out of sight, probably settling on his thigh.

They're cute together.

And cute only in the sense that they look good sitting next to each other. Because the kiss Tony and I witnessed when we were walking up to the restaurant was anything but cute. They didn't even notice us crossing the street a dozen paces away.

I'm not gonna try to steal her, but I had to shake my leg as we entered the restaurant, jostling things back into place.

"So." Tony drums his fingers on the table after the server leaves with our orders. "Waller told me you two met in college."

Hannah blushes.

Maddox answers. "She spotted me across the quad and obviously became obsessed."

Hannah shakes her head, biting her lower lip. "Not exactly. But" — her gaze moves over to meet mine — "I think you were there. That first time I saw Maddox."

I sit up straighter. "Me?"

She nods. "I'm pretty sure it was you trying to jump on his back."

"Sounds about right," Maddox huffs, looking at me. "You're probably the reason my lower back always fucking hurts."

"Yeah, it was definitely me. And not you constantly bashing your big ass into other guys every week."

Tony snorts. "Fucking athletes."

Hannah turns to Tony. "I take it you didn't play with these guys."

"Nah, I met Waller at a dinner like this, actually. Friend of a friend sorta thing." He gestures at the table.

"And since Waller and Maddox are such fucking bosom buddies, they became a throuple," Max snarks from my other side.

I lunge for him, trying to shove my finger in his ear, but the fucker darts his head out of the way.

"That training must be working." I sit back. "You're getting quicker."

Max rolls his neck. "That's true, but you're also old and out of shape."

I scoff and push my chest out. "Who you callin' out of shape?"

At just that time, the server returns with our drinks, setting the beer down in front of me first.

Max lifts a brow, like me drinking a beer proves his point.

I lift my glass with one hand and flip him off with the other. "Enjoy your water, loser."

I'm pretty sure Max is already twenty-one, but he's gearing up for his senior season down in Arizona with hopes of getting drafted next spring, so good on him for abstaining.

Tony gets some type of dark liquor in a glass with one giant ice cube, and then the server presents a bottle of white wine to Maddox before pouring a glass each for him and Hannah, leaving the bottle on the table.

Another server shows up with a plate of homemade crackers and butter while Tony tells some story, but I'm too distracted watching Maddox and Hannah to listen.

NINETY-SIX
HANNAH

We all shift our drinks around to make room, and the server sets down the final dish.

This restaurant serves food family style, and with any other group, I'd say we ordered too much. But I've seen Maddox eat, and I have a feeling the rest of these guys are the same.

Maddox scoops some of everything onto my plate first, then everyone digs in.

The first bites are delicious.

I've been meaning to try this place out, and I'm happy it's living up to its reputation.

Another forkful, and I have to stop myself from exclaiming how good everything is.

And while Max tells Waller about his summer workouts, I take another sip of wine. It's just as wonderful as everything else, but... I take another sip. It's familiar.

Reaching out, I turn the wine bottle so it's facing me.

My brows furrow.

The design is simple. A thin line borders the square sticker,

The man in question looks over his shoulder at me. And smiles.

I blush.

Keeping my eyes down, I take my seat, and Maddox pushes my chair in. But just as he promised, none of them say anything suggestive or act weird about our absence.

The conversation picks back up, the guys talking about football and coaches and other things while I finish what's on my plate.

Maddox pours me another glass of wine, and I savor every sip. Thinking of him thinking of me as I absorb the flavors.

Max is really nice, definitely a Lovelace, and I feel a little bad for not talking to any of them more, but they all seem so comfortable together, so I decide just to enjoy the atmosphere.

"You still got that old-ass car?" Max asks, setting his fork down and leaning back in his chair.

Tony scoffs. "You mispronounced classic. And you're just jealous."

Max rolls his eyes. "Sorry, but the car of my dreams gets more than four miles to the gallon."

Tony tips his head toward Maddox. "Maybe I should invest in some solar energy to offset my footprint."

"If you want to give me money, just say so." Maddox smirks at Tony, then turns to Max. "As soon as you're drafted, I'm setting you up with my financial adviser. Mrs. Hunt knows her way around a sports contract, and if you listen to her, you won't blow through your cash like so many guys do."

Waller nods. "So true. And then you can move back home and buy a business like us."

"Yeah, please, let me be one of the three musketeers," Max deadpans.

Not wanting to remain completely silent, I focus on Waller. "You own a company here too?"

"I do." His grin catches me off guard. "It's not far from your offices, actually. Maybe you've heard of it. Catch Tech."

My mouth opens, because that does sound familiar, but then my mouth snaps shut because I remember why.

I applied for a job there.

Recently.

But he wouldn't know that, would he? He's the owner, so it's not like he'd look at new résumés... Right?

Then Waller winks at me.

My face flushes, and Maddox exhales — loudly.

Wait, does Maddox know?!

The server appears to save us all, cutting in so I don't have to ask or answer any Catch Tech–related questions.

"Would anyone like to see the dessert menu?" The server addresses the table.

The question reminds me, and I answer for everyone. "No, thank you."

The server nods and clears a stack of empty plates off the table, then leaves.

Tony chuckles. "You sick of us already, Hannah?"

"No, sorry." I apologize while reaching for my purse under my chair. "I should've let you guys answer, but it's just... I brought something."

I set the Tupperware on the table where my plate had been.

Then I think about what I'm doing and press my hands down on the lid. "Maybe I should've asked if they allow outside food."

Maddox pulls the container out from under my hands. "No one is gonna tell us no. What did you —" He pulls the lid off and stops talking.

"Mom and Chelsea made them," I say quietly.

Maddox stares at the pile of jerseys. The red and yellow frosting is bright, even in the dimly lit restaurant.

"Babe." His voice sounds scratchier than it did a moment ago.

I lift a shoulder. "They made them while wearing their new jerseys."

A big arm slings around my shoulders and pulls me toward him.

My chair starts to tip, and someone — Max — on the other side of me, presses it back down.

"Christ, man, you almost knocked her over," Max snaps.

But Maddox is busy pressing his lips against the top of my head.

Bent over, I reach into the container and take out the cookie with the number nineteen piped on it. Max's number.

I pass it over to Max as Maddox finally lets me go.

"What's this?" Max stares down at the cookie.

"My niece made it for you. She googled your number and said you'd probably play for the Biters soon anyway."

Max looks up at me, then back to the cookie, then over to Maddox. "Kiss her again."

ONE HUNDRED TWO
MADDOX

I don't often listen to my little brother, but in this case, I do as he says and pull Hannah back to me. Only this time, I press my lips to hers.

"You're the fucking best," I tell her, with my lips still against hers.

"I didn't do anything. When I got home from work yesterday, they were already decorating them."

"Doesn't matter." I kiss her once more, then let her go.

Waller is leaning over the table, reaching into the container. I yank it away.

"Hey!" he complains.

"These are mine."

"Max got one," Waller argues.

"That one had Max's number on it." I look over and see Max taking a photo of the cookie.

"We can make more." Hannah tries to pacify me. "I brought these to share."

"Yeah, you should share," Tony says with his mouth full.

The elevator doors slide open, and I smile as I step off onto my floor, typing the last text while I walk toward my office.

> Me: I'm at the office. Please try not to die today.

Slipping my phone into my purse, I return hellos as I walk down the hall.

It's only been a few days since I saw Maddox.

Since the dinner.

Since we fell asleep together in my small bed.

Since I woke up alone.

Just a few days, but still far too long.

When I first found out Maddox was the new owner, all I wanted was for him not to be in the office. But now I dread the days he's not here.

I drop all my stuff on my desk and turn back around, heading to the break room.

I didn't bring lunch today, figured I'd eat my feelings with some takeout, but I still need my coffee.

Donut Guy is in his usual spot, but other than him, the room is empty.

Maddox has made me coffee a few times, and it's always been in the same handmade mug, so I select that one from the cupboard and set it on the counter.

I pour my coffee, then turn to get my creamer from the fridge and jump.

Brandon is there. Standing at the fridge, his cotton candy drink in hand.

"Oh, hey, Brandon." I press my hand over my heart. "You startled me."

"Oops." His tone is flat, and instead of saying more — bothering me like he usually does — he turns and walks toward the door.

Well, that was uncomfortable.

The part of me controlled by society feels a little bad about telling him I have a boyfriend. But the rest of me realizes that's fucking nonsense.

He's done nothing to be considerate of my boundaries.

He's never taken one single hint that I'm not interested.

He's pushed himself into my space more times than I can count.

He's been a constant annoyance and, worse than that, a threat since I started. Because women in the workplace are so easily labeled as *difficult to work with*. We're chastised for being *too sensitive* when a man says something grossly offensive and inappropriate to us. We're meant to *laugh with them* when they make derogatory comments about other women in front of us. We're supposed to put up with so much motherfucking shit from men and not do anything about it for fear of losing our jobs. All while the worst men can't rub two brain cells together to consider that maybe they're the hard ones to work with. That maybe *they* need to take a moment to think before they speak. Their egos are the largest hindrance to progress. That maybe their biggest worry is absolutely trivial compared to our biggest worries.

I heave out a breath and remind myself I won't stay here much longer.

Brandon's behavior didn't really get any worse after Maddox bought the company; it's just that Maddox is everything Brandon isn't. And it shows just how predatory Brandon has been.

Pulling my half-and-half out of the fridge, I turn toward my coffee.

Toward my memories of Maddox.

Toward thoughts of a man who respects women.

And I forget all about Brandon and his hurt little feelings.

I turn back to Brenda. "You the one supervising me?"

She nods.

I stand. "Let's get this over with then."

MADDOX

Me: I survived.

Bunny: I'm glad to hear it.

Me: How's your day going? What did you get for lunch?

Bunny: I'm about to eat a burrito, meaning my day is about to get better.

Me: Sounds delicious. But not as delicious as you.

ONE HUNDRED TEN
HANNAH

I set my phone down on the passenger seat of my car and pull out of the company parking lot.

I'm not happy about getting fired. But I don't regret anything. Having Maddox Lovelace back in my life is exactly what I didn't know I needed. And I wouldn't give him up for anything.

I do need a job though.

As I come to a red light, a thought strikes me.

ONE HUNDRED ELEVEN
NATE WALLER

"Mr. Waller?" the summer intern sticks his head into my office.

"Yeah?" I manage not to sigh. Clearly this kid is never gonna just call me Waller.

"There's someone on the phone for you. Her name is, uh" — he looks at the note in his hand — "Hannah Utley."

I lean forward in my chair. "Put her through."

The second my phone rings, I answer it. "Hannah?"

"Hi, um, Waller?"

"It's me. Is something wrong?" I can't keep the edge of panic out of my voice. Maddox is my best friend, and if something happened to him...

"No. No, I promise, Maddox is fine." She reads my mind.

I heave out a breath and sink back into my chair. "Fuck. I'm too young for a heart attack."

Her laughter sounds as stressed as I feel. "Sorry, I wasn't thinking. Should've opened with *Maddox is alive and well.*"

"No, no, you're good." I wave her off even though she can't see me. "That blockhead will outlive us all. So, if it's not Maddox, what's up?"

We only met the one time, over dinner this week, but by the time we parted ways, I knew I liked her. And I knew Maddox would marry her.

"Well, I don't really know how to ask this..." She still sounds stressed.

I'm back to sitting upright. "For the sake of my cardiac health, please just ask it."

"Okay." Her exhale scratches across the phone. "Do you still have that position open?"

My brain mentally blinks at her question. *Position?*

"The job? Here?" I ask, finally remembering her résumé that's still in my desk somewhere.

"If not, that's totally okay. I just thought I'd ask," she rushes out.

"Why are you asking? Did Maddox do something stupid?"

Hannah's laugh is more natural this time. "No, it's, well, I got fired today."

My eyes widen. "Maddox fired you?"

Her scoff is instant. "No. And he's going to lose his shit when he finds out. But I can't have him just rehire me."

I shake my head even as she says it. "Yeah, best intentions and all that."

"Exactly." There's a pause. "Maybe it's dumb of me to reach out to you for those same reasons. If the spot is even still open, people might assume I got it because I'm dating your friend. Even though, I have to add, I'm more than qualified."

It's my turn to laugh. "I know you are. I was gonna call you in for an interview before I realized who you were."

"You were?"

"Yup." I tap my fingers on the desk. "But then I called Maddox, and he told me I couldn't hire you. But that was when he was still —" I cut myself off, not sure how much I should say. "But if you're no longer working for him..."

"Considering I just got escorted out of the building, I think it's safe to say I no longer work at MinneSolar." I can hear her smile. "So... is the position still open?"

I grin. "The position is still open."

In front of me, the door opens, and Chelsea appears.

"Jeez, chill, man." She's looking up at me like I've lost my mind.

And I feel like I have.

"Smidge." I try to keep my tone calm. "Where's your aunt?"

Ruth steps up behind her. "Sorry, she's gone."

I shake my head. "She can't be gone."

"Maddox —"

"I'm not letting her go."

Ruth reaches over Chelsea and smacks me lightly on the chest. "Hun, pay attention."

I blink.

Ruth smiles and lifts her hand. "She's right there."

Turning to follow her finger, I see Hannah's car turn into the driveway. And I bound down the steps.

ONE HUNDRED FIFTEEN
HANNAH

Guilt swamps me as I see the distress on Maddox's face as he practically runs toward me.

I hurry to unbuckle and get out of the car before Maddox can reach me, but by the time I have my door open, he's already there, tugging me up and out of the seat.

He slides his hands up my arms until he's palming the front of my throat in that way I love, tangling his other hand in my hair.

"I'm not letting you go, Little Bunny." His words crash into me. "Not now. Not fucking ever."

Emotions swirl my vision, and I reach up to grip his forearms. "Maddox —"

He shakes his head. "Let me say this."

I swallow and nod, the movement small with his hold on me.

"I love you, Hannah Utley. And I don't believe in curses." I grip his arms tighter. "But I'd still do it. I'd still love you, even if it kills me because I don't know any other way to live."

Tears fall freely from my eyes.

He leans down, kissing my cheek. "Don't cry, Babe." He kisses the other cheek, catching another tear on his lips. "I'll fix it."

I shake my head.

"I promise I'll fix it," he tells me again, his tone full of conviction.

"Maddox." My voice breaks.

His hand leaves my hair so he can brush his thumb under my eye. "You're not fired, Hannah Bunny. I won't let them."

God, this man.

I shake my head, but he shakes his own.

"It's my company. I can change the rules."

I release one of his arms so I can press my palm against his chest, over his heart. "Maddox, I can't work for you. I'm not coming back."

"I —" he starts, then I watch him fight through a swallow. "I know you're talking about work, but I can't hear you say that. I can't hear you say you're not coming back."

"Oh, Maddox." I press my palm against him harder. "I'm not leaving you. Not ever. Not like that. I just can't work for you. I love you too much." His chest hitches under my touch. "I'm sorry I didn't tell you when it all happened on Friday. I should have. I just... I didn't want you to feel like you'd need to fix it."

He flexes his fingers around my neck. "Say it again."

"I'm sorry —"

Maddox shakes his head as he leans in closer. "The other part, Hannah. Say the other part again."

My lips form a soft smile. "I love you, Maddox Lovelace. Have for a long time."

He lowers his mouth to mine.

It's not frantic. Not rough. But it's still a claiming.

His lips press against mine. Warm and coaxing. Asking me again to tell him that I love him.

So I do.

I open for him.

I let him taste me as I taste him back.

He wraps his arms around me, and I do the same, reaching my arms up around his neck.

Maddox tightens his grip and lifts me off the ground, my toes dangling inches above the blacktop.

"Tell me again," I whisper between kisses.

"I love you, Hannah. Have for a long time."

I roll my hips, arching my back.

Maddox pushes his third finger inside me as he drags the tip of his cock up my crack, my wetness spreading with the movement.

No one has ever touched me back there before, and the sensation is like nothing I've experienced.

He rubs the tip of his dick against the sensitive spot, and I can't stop my moan.

"Such a good girl." He shoves his trio of fingers deeper inside me, and I almost collapse.

His chuckle vibrates against my back.

"Walk forward," he commands me. "Hands on the wall, Hannah."

My knees feel like jelly, but I shuffle forward. Each step causes my core to clench around his thick fingers.

I slap my hands against the cool shower wall.

Maddox slowly drags his fingers out from inside me. But instead of moving to my breasts, he slides them around my hip and across my ass until they're... there. Where the head of his cock had been. Teasing my back entrance.

I let my head drop between my arms.

His fingers slide up and down, stimulating and setting my nerves on fire. And then the head of his dick nudges against my core.

"I wonder." He notches his cock inside me and slowly pushes an inch into my pussy.

We both moan.

"I wonder." He tries again. "If you'd still like my thick fingers if I put them here." One fingertip presses harder.

I can't help it.

I arch into the feeling, sliding his cock deeper into me.

Maddox makes a sound low in his throat. "You would, wouldn't you?"

He doesn't push his finger into me, just wiggles it. Right. There.

"I bet you'd come so hard, with my cock filling your pussy and my finger filling your ass."

Holy fuck. Why is that so hot?

He thrusts his hips forward, and I cry out.

His cock is still bigger than three of his fingers, and the intrusion is always overwhelming.

He drags himself out, then thrusts in again.

"Maddox!"

He does it again. "That's right. It's me inside you." He moves his finger in a circle. "It will only ever be me inside you."

His dick throbs so hard I can feel it. And I know he's got to be close.

I bend over farther. Taking him deeper.

His cock drags over a spot inside me, and I jolt.

He does it again, and I squeeze.

He does it again, and I'm almost there.

"So close." I choke on the words. "I'm so close."

He tilts his hips, and the pressure increases. "Touch yourself. Get yourself there, Hannah. Because I'm about to paint this ass with my cum."

I shove my hand down between my legs. I don't ease into anything. I just rub frantically at my clit.

So close.

I'm so close.

He drags his cock almost all the way out. And it's all I need.

My orgasm grips me and drags me under.

I tense and throw my head back.

I think I say his name.

I think tears leak from my eyes.

Maddox shouts something, then he's as deep as he can get.

I feel him pulse.

Feel him start to fill me.

Then he's gone.

His cock is pulled out of me.

Fingers dig into the flesh of my ass as he spreads me, exposes me, and I feel heat.

Hot splashes of his release over my ass, across my lower back, between my legs.

He's making more sounds.

Saying things that sound like praise.

But I can't hear anything over the hum in my ears.

And when I feel like I might collapse, strong arms circle my waist, keeping me from falling.

ONE HUNDRED TWENTY
HANNAH

I eye the pile of clothes on the bed.

Maddox got out of the shower first, telling me to take my time and that he'd put comfortable clothes out for me on the bed.

He did.

But they're... well, they aren't *mine*. But they certainly aren't his.

It's a soft jersey dress in dark blue, a pair of panties, and a matching bra. All in my size.

I have no idea when he got these, but I pull the items on, preferring them to the stuffy work clothes I was wearing.

I'm pulling my hair free from the dress's collar when I spot something orange on the nightstand.

It's a thing of Tic Tacs, just sitting out. Next to the lamp.

I pick it up and shake two into my palm.

Did he remember from before? Or from our kiss inside his car, when he put his mouth against mine for the first time since before?

I've always liked these. We had them in the study room that night. I have them in my purse now too.

Setting the little container down, I suck on the tiny candies and turn around toward the door.

But again. I stop.

When we first got here, the room seemed brighter, but I credited that to my racing heart. And when we woke up just a bit ago, the sun was shining through the windows, and I associated the brightness with the sunlight.

But it's not just the sun making a difference. The walls are a different color.

I step closer, reaching out to touch the pale yellow surface.

Maddox had the bedroom painted? When?

My eyes move to the four large black square frames mounted on the wall that I swear weren't there before.

Inside each frame is a black and white photograph.

I move to them, and that feeling of tenderness tightens around my throat.

It's the HOP University campus.

A photo of the quad. Where I first saw Maddox.

A photo of the economics building. Where I ran into Maddox.

A photo of the football stadium. Where I watched my first game.

A photo of the library. Where we shared our first everything.

I press my hand to my chest.

"When?" I ask the question to the empty room.

This man...

I hurry out of the room, needing to be near him.

When I reach the bottom of the stairs, I release the banister and eye the fresh flowers displayed on the small antique table.

Has that little table always been there?

What is happening in this house?

I hear movement as I near the kitchen and find Maddox closing the fridge.

"Hey, when did you..." I trail off.

On the island, next to another bouquet of flowers, is the yellow mug from the office. The one I used on Friday.

Then I step closer.

It's not the same one. The yellow glaze is slightly darker.

Pinpricks dance across my ribs. "Where did you get this?"

When Maddox doesn't answer, I glance up to see him sipping out of an identical mug, only his is blue.

"Ordered them online," he answers, then dips his head to the mug on the counter. "I made it decaf, but I can make you some regular coffee if you'd like."

I stare at the mug. Then I stare up at him.

"Maddox, what is —"

The doorbell rings.

Maddox smiles at me as he sets his coffee mug down next to mine. "I'll get that."

He presses a kiss to my forehead, then walks past me to answer the door.

I look back at the mugs. Then to the flowers.

With my heart thudding, I move around the island and pull open the cupboard where he keeps his dishes.

Everything is different.

The mugs are all handmade. The cups are no longer all the same plain glass but rather antique looking with raised polka dots on the sides. The serving dishes are pieces of art.

I love every item. It's exactly what I'd get if we had the space and money.

I close the cupboard and step back.

Mom's voice echoes through the house, followed by a laugh that could only belong to Chelsea.

I plan to go and meet them, but then I see the living room. And the now familiar sense of surprise thumps against my chest.

The couch, which is nice but had previously been bare, is covered in throw pillows of all colors and sizes. Blankets are folded on the coffee table alongside another vase, this one over-flowing with roses.

And under the coffee table is a new massive rug. It's plush and red, and I want to walk on it.

But as I cross the room to do just that, I see more.

On the end table, hanging off the side lamp, is a necklace. A tacky plastic necklace made of little baseballs.

I can't fight against my tears any longer.

My eyes fill and spill over.

"Come on into the kitchen," Maddox says as their footsteps enter the large space.

"Hey, Aunt Hannah."

I lift my hand but keep my back to them for another second. "Hey."

"I have different cans of pop and tea and stuff in the fridge," Maddox tells them. "Help yourself."

"Thank you." Mom's voice is full of smiles. "Oh, look at these flowers! I just love flowers."

"I know," Maddox replies, but he says it quietly from behind me.

I turn, wiping at my eyes. "What is going on?"

His smile is soft, and he holds his hand out to me. "Let me show you."

I slide my palm into his. "Show me what?"

Maddox lifts my hand and kisses it gently. "The rest of it." He turns, and I move with him. "You guys want the tour?"

Chelsea nods as her eyes bounce around the giant kitchen.

Maddox points at things, and Mom makes sounds of enjoyment.

He takes us to the basement and shows us the gym and the movie room.

He walks us around the main level.

Chelsea gives me the side-eye each time I sniffle. Each time I see another item that has to be new. Each time we come across another collection of fresh flowers.

Finally, we move up the staircase to the upper level. But Maddox doesn't let go of my hand. He hasn't this whole time. And when we reach the top of the stairs, he squeezes my fingers.

He points toward his room. "That's the way to the owner's suite. But this way" — he points in the other direction — "is the next stop on our tour."

Mom and Chelsea turn and walk ahead of us.

The first guest room door is open, and Mom steps through.

When I hear her gasp, I look up at Maddox. And he's already looking down at me.

"Oh, wow." Mom keeps talking as she moves deeper into the room.

Chelsea steps into the doorway, then glances back at us.

I have to know.

Keeping hold of Maddox's hand, I move toward the guest room.

A room that should be painted white.

A room that should be nice but plain and unused.

A room that shouldn't be painted a gentle lilac.

A room that shouldn't have floral bedding and grand antique furniture.

A room that shouldn't have potted blooming plants filling the windowsill.

EPILOGUE 2 – MADDOX

Pride fills my chest as I look down at the field.

As Chelsea predicted, Max got drafted by the Minnesota Biters, and today is his first pro ball game.

Hannah comes to stand on my right, at the front of the private suite we're watching the game from. "Nervous?"

I drape my arm over her shoulders and pull her into my side. "Nah. He's not starting, so he probably won't play."

She rests her head against my chest. "I'm proud of him too."

I tighten my hold on her.

It's September. Just over a year since we found each other again, and my love for this woman has only grown.

I lift my left hand and wiggle my fingers, watching the light glint off the silver band on my third finger.

After I proposed, we started looking at wedding venues. But when I realized how far out they were booking, I told Hannah I couldn't wait anymore. So we went to the courthouse. And with Ruth, Chelsea, Max, Waller, and my parents in tow, we got married.

Tony comes up from behind me and slaps my hand down.

"How about you stop reminding me that you didn't invite me to your wedding."

I roll my eyes. "I've told you a thousand times, you didn't answer your phone. But you're already invited to the reception we're planning next summer."

He scoffs. "I'm no horologist, but aren't weddings and receptions at the same time, not a year something apart?"

I slowly turn my head to face him. "A horologist?"

Waller comes up behind us. "Why are we talking about the study of time?"

I stare at my friends, wondering why I like them.

"Down in front!" Chelsea pushes her way past Waller to stand next to Tony. "Chivalry is dead."

Waller clutches his chest. "You wound me."

"Uh-huh." The teen ignores him, used to his bullshit by now.

We stay where we are, standing together as a group, my parents somewhere nearby, as the game starts.

We start on defense, and I can't help but watch how the tackles handle themselves.

The Biters have been building a team for years, getting better the longer they play together.

It's a *good news, bad news* thing for Max.

Good news is he's on a team with a winning trajectory.

Bad news because unless something happens to the starting quarterback, he won't get field time.

The other team doesn't score, and now it's our turn at offense.

The return on the kick is good, and the Biters line up for their first down at a decent yard line.

The ball is snapped. The quarterback is looking. And a defensive tackle slips through the line.

From above, we watch it happen.

The hit.
The bodies going down.
The arm bending the wrong way.
Our starting quarterback is hurt.
He's out.
And Max is in.

ABOUT THE AUTHOR

S.J. Tilly was born and raised in Minnesota, but now calls Colorado her home.

When she's not busy writing her contemporary smut, she can be found lounging with her husband and their herd of rescue boxers.

To stay up to date on all things Tilly, make sure to follow her on her socials, join her newsletter, and interact whenever you feel like it! Links to everything on her website www.sjtilly.com

ALSO BY S.J. TILLY

Love Letters Series
Contemporary Romance

Love, Utley
Hannah

Maddox Lovelace. The captivating football player I met in college.

The one I only knew for a week. A week that was... life-changing.

Until my phone rang, and I had no choice but to go home.

I left Maddox a letter, putting my feelings on paper, giving him my number, hoping he'd call.

But he didn't call.

He never called.

He got drafted into the professional league and lived like a king while I stayed home and struggled to stay afloat.

I may have followed his career, but now that he's retired from football, I've forced myself to stop thinking about him.

And it's okay that I won't ever see him again. That week in college was fifteen years ago.

I'm not in love with Maddox anymore.

I might even hate him.

Maddox

Hannah Utley. The name that's haunted me since my senior year of college.

The girl who caught my attention with her wide eyes and freckled nose.

Who spent one week twisting up my insides until she stole a piece of my heart the night we got locked inside the campus library.

The girl who disappeared without a word.

It's the name of the girl I've been trying to forget for fifteen years.

And it's the name looking up at me from the résumé in my hand.

Because Hannah Utley works for the company I just purchased.

And that makes her mine. Whether she likes it or not.

Alliance Series
Dark Mafia Romance

NERO

Payton

Running away from home at seventeen wasn't easy. Let's face it, though, nothing before, or in the ten years since, has ever been easy for me.

And I'm doing okay. Sorta. I just need to keep scraping by, living under the radar. Staying out of people's way, off people's minds.

So when a man walks through my open patio door, stepping boldly into my home and my life, I should be scared. Frightened. Terrified.

But I must be more broken than I realized because I'm none of those things.

I'm intrigued.

And I'm wondering if the way to take control of my life is by giving in to him.

Nero

The first time I took a man's life, I knew there'd be no going back. No normal existence in the cards for me.

So instead of walking away, I climbed a mountain of bodies and created my own destiny. By forming The Alliance.

And I was fine with that. Content enough to carry on.

Until I stepped through those open doors and into her life.

I should've walked away. Should've gone right back out the door I came through. But I didn't.

And now her life is in danger.

But that's the thing about being a bad man. I'll happily paint the streets red to protect what's mine.

And Payton is mine. Whether she knows it or not.

KING

Okay, so, my bad for assuming the guy I was going on a date with *wasn't* married. And my bad for taking him to a friend's house for dinner, only to find out my friend is also friends with *his* wife. Because, in fact, he *is* married. And she happens to be at my friend's house because her husband was *busy working*.

Confused? So am I.

Unsurprisingly, my date's wife is super angry about finding out that her husband is a cheating asshole.

Girl, I get it.

Then, to make matters more convoluted, there is the man sitting next to my date's wife. A man named King, who is apparently her brother and who lives up to his name.

And since my *date* is a two-timing prick, I'm not going to feel bad about drooling over King,

especially since I'll never see him again.

Or at least I don't plan to.

I plan to take an Uber to the cheater's apartment to get my car keys.

I plan for it to be quick.

And if I had to list a thousand possible outcomes... witnessing my date's murder, being kidnapped by his killer, and then being forced to marry the super attractive but clearly

deranged crime lord would not have been on my Bingo card.

But alas, here I am.

DOM

VAL

When I was nine, I went to my first funeral. Along with accepting my father's death, I had to accept new and awful truths I wasn't prepared for.

When I was nineteen, I went to my mother's funeral. We weren't close, but with her gone, I became more alone than ever before.

Sure, I have a half brother who runs The Alliance. And yeah, he's given me his protection—in the form of a bodyguard and chauffeur. But I don't have anyone that really knows me. No one to really love me.

Until I meet him. The man in the airport.

And when one chance meeting turns into something hotter, something more serious, I let myself believe that maybe he's the one. Maybe this man is the one who will finally save me from my loneliness. The one to give me the family I've always craved.

DOM

The Mafia is in my blood. It's what I do.

So when that blood is spilled and one funeral turns into three, drastic measures need to be taken.

And when this battle turns into a war, I'm going to need more men.
More power.

I'm going to need The Alliance.

And I'll become a member. By any means necessary.

HANS

Cassie

How to make the handsome, brooding man across the street notice me.

Step one: Deliver baked goods to his front porch, even though he never answers his door and always returns the containers when I'm not home.

Step two: Slowly lose my mind as a whole year passes without ever running into him, no matter how hard I try.

Step three: Have my boudoir photos accidentally delivered to his mailbox instead of mine. Have him open the package. Then have him storm into my home for the most panty-melting scolding of my life.

Step four: Still figuring out step four.

Hans

I'm a dangerous man.

A man who has spent the last two decades removing so many souls from this earth that it's a miracle my hands aren't permanently stained red.

I'm a man who belongs in the shadows.

I certainly don't belong in my pretty little neighbor's bedroom when she's not home, touching her things and inhaling her scent.

I shouldn't follow her. Shouldn't watch her. Because no number of cookies on my doorstep will change the fact that love isn't an option for me.

The only option left for me is violence.

Sin Series

Romantic Suspense

Mr. Sin

I should have run the other way. Paid my tab and gone back to my room. But he was there. And he was... everything. I figured, what's the harm in letting passion rule my decisions for one night? So what if he looks like the Devil in a suit? I'd be leaving in the morning. Flying home, back to my pleasant but predictable life. I'd never see him again.

Except I do. In the last place I expected. And now everything I've worked so hard for is in jeopardy.

We can't stop what we've started, but this is bigger than the two of us.

And when his past comes back to haunt him, love might not be enough to save me.

Sin Too

Beth

It started with tragedy.

And secrets.

Hidden truths that refused to stay buried have come out to chase me. Now I'm on the run, living under a blanket of constant fear, pretending to be someone I'm not. And if I'm not really me, how am I supposed to know what's real?

Angelo

Watch the girl.

It was supposed to be a simple assignment. But like everything else in this family, there's nothing simple about it. Not my task. Not her fake name. And not my feelings for her.

But Beth is mine now.

So when the monsters from her past come out to play, they'll have to get through me first.

Miss Sin

I'm so sick of watching the world spin by. Of letting people think I'm plain and boring, too afraid to just be myself.

Then I see *him*.

John.

He's strength and fury and unapologetic.

He's everything I want. And everything I wish I was.

He won't want me, but that doesn't matter. The sight of him is all the inspiration I need to finally shatter this glass house I've built around myself.

Only he does want me. And when our worlds collide, details we can't see become tangled, twisting together, ensnaring us in an invisible trap.

When it all goes wrong, I don't know if I'll be able to break free of the chains binding us or if I'll suffocate in the process.

Sleet Series

Hockey Romantic Comedy

Sleet Kitten

There are a few things that life doesn't prepare you for. Like what to do when a super-hot guy catches you sneaking around in his basement. Or what to do when a mysterious package shows up with tickets to a hockey game, because apparently, he's a professional athlete. Or how to handle it when you get to the game and realize he's freaking famous since half of the 20,000 people in the stands are wearing his jersey.

I thought I was a well-adjusted adult, reasonably prepared for life. But one date with Jackson Wilder, a viral video, and a "I didn't know she was your mom" incident, and I'm suddenly questioning everything I thought I knew.

But he's fun. And great. And I think I might be falling for him. But I don't know if he's falling for me too, or if he's as much of a player off the ice as on.

Sleet Sugar

My friends have convinced me. No more hockey players.

With a dad who is the head coach for the Minnesota Sleet, it seemed like an easy decision.

My friends have also convinced me that the best way to boost my fragile self-esteem is through a one-night stand.

A dating app. A hotel bar. A sexy-as-hell man, who's sweet and funny, and did I mention, sexy as hell... I fortified my courage and invited myself up to his room.

Assumptions. There's a rule about them.

I assumed he was passing through town. I assumed he was a businessman or maybe an investor or accountant or literally anything other than a professional hockey player. I assumed I'd never see him again.

I assumed wrong.

Sleet Banshee

Mother-freaking hockey players. My friends found their happily ever afters with a couple of sweet, doting, over-the-top, in-love athletes. They got nicknames like *Kitten* and *Sugar*. But me? I got stuck with a dickhead who riles me up on purpose and calls me *Banshee*. Yeah, he might have a voice made specifically for wet dreams. And he might have a body and face carved by the gods. And he might have a level of Alpha-hole that gets me all hot and bothered.

But when he presses my buttons, he presses ALL of my buttons. And I'm not the type of girl who takes things sitting down. And I only got caught on my knees that one time. In the museum.

But when one of my decisions gets one of my friends hurt... I can't stop blaming myself. And him.

Except he can't take a hint. And I can't keep my panties on.

Sleet Princess

My trip to Mexico for my cousin's wedding was only supposed to be a few days of obligation and oceanside.

I wasn't expecting Luke.

Wasn't expecting the hot hockey player, with the smirks and the tattoos, who kept *bumping into me*.

And I certainly wasn't expecting to spend a night on the beach, under the stars, underneath *him*.

It was magical, but I thought it would end there.

Instead, we exchanged numbers and stayed in touch.

So when Luke invited me to watch him play in Vegas, I went.

And it was great.

Until we woke up the next morning and found the wedding certificate in my pocket.

Turns out that dance party we snuck into was actually a group wedding ceremony.

And now we're married.

Which is bad.

Because I think our wedding was actually our first date. And if my dad finds out, he'll cut me out of the family business.

So when footage leaks of Luke and me hot and heavy in an elevator, I have to make up a new plan to save my reputation and career.

Now, all I need is for Luke Anders to act like he's madly in love with me.

Should be easy.

Right?

Darling Series

Contemporary Small Town Romance

Smoky Darling

Elouise

I fell in love with Beckett when I was seven.

He broke my heart when I was fifteen.

When I was eighteen, I promised myself I'd forget about him.

And I did. For a dozen years.

But now he's back home. Here. In Darling Lake. And I don't know if I should give in to the temptation swirling between us or run the other way.

Beckett

She had a crush on me when she was a kid. But she was my brother's best friend's little sister. I didn't see her like that. And even if I had, she was too young. Our age difference was too great.

But now I'm back home. And she's here. And she's all the way grown up.

It wouldn't have worked back then. But I'll be damned if I won't get a taste of her now.

Latte Darling

I have a nice life—living in my hometown, owning the coffee shop I've worked at since I was sixteen.

It's comfortable.

On paper.

But I'm tired of doing everything by myself. Tired of being in charge of every decision in my life.

I want someone to lean on. Someone to spend time with. Sit with. Hug.

And I really don't want to go to my best friend's wedding alone.

So, I signed up for a dating app and agreed to meet with the first guy who messaged me.

And now here I am, at the bar.

Only it's not my date that just sat down in the chair across from me. It's his dad.

And holy hell, he's the definition of silver fox. If a silver fox can be thick as a house, have piercing blue eyes and tattoos from his neck down to his fingertips.

He's giving me *big bad wolf* vibes. Only instead of running, I'm blushing. And he looks like he might just want to eat me whole.

Tilly World Holiday Novellas
Second Bite

When a holiday baking competition goes incredibly wrong. Or right...

Michael

I'm starting to think I've been doing this for too long. The screaming fans. The constant media attention. The fat paychecks. None of it brings me the happiness I yearn for.

Yet here I am. Another year. Another holiday special. Another Christmas spent alone in a hotel room.

But then the lights go up. And I see *her*.

Alice

It's an honor to be a contestant, I know that. But right now, it feels a little like punishment. Because any second, Chef Michael Kesso, the man I've been in love with for years, the man who doesn't even know I exist, is going to walk onto the set, and it will be a miracle if I don't pass out at the sight of him.

But the time for doubts is over. Because *Second Bite* is about to start "in three... two... one..."